Lucy Temple

Lucy Temple
Susanna Rowson

MINT EDITIONS

Lucy Temple was first published in 1871.

This edition published by Mint Editions 2021.

ISBN 9781513291963 | E-ISBN 9781513294810

Published by Mint Editions®

 MINT
EDITIONS
minteditionbooks.com

Publishing Director: Jennifer Newens
Design & Production: Rachel Lopez Metzger
Project Manager: Micaela Clark
Typesetting: Westchester Publishing Services

Contents

I. False Pride and Unsophisticated Innocence   7

II. The Little Heiress, and the Master of the Mansion   10

III. The Three Orphans   14

IV. Romance, Piety, Sensibility   18

V. A Lesson, Change of Scene   30

VI. A Rencontre, A Balls Love at First Sight   38

VII. Folly, Rectitude, A Visit to Serjeant Blandford   45

VIII. Unpleasant Discovery—Bitter Repentance   57

IX. The Letter—the Birth-day   66

X. Manœuvring—establishment Formed—Change of Circumstances Alters Cases   77

XI. Fruits of Error   84

XII. Disclosures   86

XIII. An Arrival   89

XIV. Active Benevolence, the Best Remedy for Affliction   91

XV. Church and State   94

XVI. An Engagement   96

XVII. Tea-Table Conversation   98

XVIII. An Adventure   100

   XIX. The Consequences of Imprudence   103

   XX. An Old-Fashioned Wedding   107

Conclusion   109

I

FALSE PRIDE AND
UNSOPHISTICATED INNOCENCE

W hat are you doing there Lucy?" said Mrs. Cavendish to a lovely girl, about fifteen years old. She was kneeling at the feet of an old man sitting just within the door of a small thatched cottage situated about five miles from Southampton on the coast of Hampshire. "What are you doing there child?" said she, in rather a sharp tone, repeating her question.

"Binding up sergeant Blandford's leg ma'am," said the kind hearted young creature, looking up in the face of the person who spoke to her. At the same time, rising on one knee, she rested the lame limb on a stool on which was a soft cushion which this child of benevolence had provided for the old soldier.

"And was there no one but you Miss Blakeney who could perform such an office? You demean yourself strangely." "I did not think it was any degradation," replied Lucy, "to perform an act of kindness to a fellow creature, but I have done now," continued she rising, "and will walk home with you ma'am if you please." She then wished the sergeant a goodnight, and tying on her bonnet which had been thrown on the floor during her employment, she took Mrs. Cavendish's arm, and they proceeded to the house of the Rector of the village.

"There! Mr. Matthews," exclaimed the lady on entering the parlor, "there! I have brought home Miss Blakeney, and where do you think I found her? and how employed?"

"Where you found her," replied Mr. Matthews, smiling, "I will not pretend to say; for she is a sad rambler, but I dare be bound that you did not find her either foolishly or improperly employed."

"I found her in old Blandford's cottage, swathing up his lame leg." "And how my good madam," inquired Mr. Matthews, "could innocence be better employed, than in administering to the comforts of the defender of his country?"

"Well, well, you always think her right, but we shall hear what my sister says to it. Mrs. Matthews, do you approve of a young lady of rank and fortune making herself familiar with all the beggars and low people in the place?"

"By no means," said the stately Mrs. Matthews, "and I am astonished that Miss Blakeney has not a higher sense of propriety and her own consequence."

"Dear me, ma'am," interrupted Lucy, "it was to make myself of consequence that I did it; for lady Mary, here at home, says I am nobody, an insignificant Miss Mushroom, but sergeant Blandford calls me his guardian angel, his comforter; and I am sure those are titles of consequence."

"Bless me," said Mrs. Cavendish, "what plebian ideas the girl has imbibed, it is lucky for you child, that you were so early removed from those people."

"I hope Madam," replied Lucy, "you do not mean to say that it was fortunate for me that I was so early deprived of the protection of my dear grandfather? Alas! it was a heavy day for me; he taught me that the only way to become of real consequence, is to be useful to my fellow creatures." Lucy put her hand before her eyes to hide the tears she could not restrain and courtesying respectfully to Mr. Matthews, his wife and sister, she left the room.

Well, I protest sister," said Mrs. Cavendish, "that is the most extraordinary girl I ever knew; with a vast number of low ideas and habits, she can sometimes assume the *hauteur* and air of a dutchess. In what a respectful yet independent manner she went out of the room.

Mrs. Matthews was too much irritated to reply with calmness, she therefore wisely continued silent. Mr. Matthews was silent from a different cause, and supper being soon after announced, the whole family went into the parlor; Lucy had dried her tears, and with a placid countenance seated herself by her reverend friend Mr. Matthews. "*You*, I hope, are not angry with me, Sir?" said she with peculiar emphasis. "No my child," he replied, pressing the hand she had laid upon his arm, "No, I am not angry, but my little Lucy must remember that she is now advancing towards womanhood, and that it is not always safe, nor perfectly proper, to be rambling about in the dusk of the evening without a companion."

"Then if you say so sir, I will never do it again; but indeed you do not know how happy my visits make old Mr. Blandford; you know, sir, he is very poor; so lady Mary would not go with me if I asked her; and he is very lame, so if Aura went with me, she is such a mad-cap, perhaps she might laugh at him; besides, when I sometimes ask Mrs. Matthews to let her walk with me, she has something for her to do, and cannot spare her."

"Well, my dear," said the kind hearted old gentleman, "when you want to visit him again ask me to go with you." "Oh! you are the best old man in the world," cried Lucy, as rising she put her arms round his neck and kissed him. "There now, there is a specimen of low breeding," said Mrs. Cavendish, "you ought to know, Miss Blakeney, that nothing can be more rude than to call a person old." "I did not mean to offend," said Lucy. "No! I am sure you did not," replied Mr. Matthews, "and so let us eat supper, for when a man or woman, sister, is turned of sixty they may be termed old, without much exaggeration, or the smallest breach of politeness."

But the reader will perhaps like to be introduced to the several individuals who compose this family.

II

The Little Heiress, and the Master
of the Mansion

Lucy Blakeney had from her earliest infancy been under the protection of her maternal grandfather; her mother had ushered her into life at the expense of her own, and captain Blakeney of the navy, having been her godfather, she was baptized by the name of Blakeney in addition to her own family name. Captain Blakeney was the intimate friend of her grandfather, he had loved her mother as his own child, and dying a bachelor when Lucy was ten years old, he left her the whole of the property he had acquired during the war which had given to the United States of America, rank and consequence among the nations of the earth; and during which period he had been fortunate in taking prizes, so that at the time of his death, his property amounted to more than twenty thousand pounds sterling. This he bequeathed to his little favorite on condition that she took the name and bore the arms of Blakeney; indeed, she had never been called by any other name, but the will required that the assumption should be legally authorized, and a further condition was, that whoever married her, should change his own family name to that of Blakeney, but on a failure of this, the original sum was to go to increase the pensions of the widows of officers of the navy dying in actual service, Lucy only retaining the interest which might have accumulated during her minority.

About two years after this rich bequest, Lucy literally became an orphan by the death of both her grandparents, within a few months of each other. She inherited from her grandfather a handsome patrimony, enough to support and educate her in a very superior style, without infringing on the bequest of captain Blakeney, the interest of which yearly accumulating would make her by the time she was twenty-one, a splendid heiress.

The reverend Mr. Matthews had lived in habits of intimacy with both the grandfather of Lucy and captain Blakeney, though considerably younger than either; he was nominated her guardian in conjunction with Sir Robert Ainslie, a banker in London, a man of strict probity, to whom the management of her fortune was intrusted.

To Mr. Matthews the care of her person was consigned, he had promised her grandfather that she should reside constantly in his family, and under his eye receive instruction in the accomplishments becoming the rank she would most probably fill in society, from the best masters; whilst the cultivation of her mental powers, the formation of her moral and religious character, and the correction of those erring propensities which are the sad inheritance of all the sons and daughters of Adam, he solemnly promised should be his own peculiar care.

Mr. Matthews was, what every minister of the Gospel should be, the profound scholar, the finished gentleman, and the sincere, devout christian. Plain and unaffected in his address to his parishioners, on the Sabbathday, or any day set apart for devotional exercises, he at all other times exemplified in his own conduct the piety and pure morality he had from the pulpit forcibly recommended to others. Liberal as far as his circumstances would allow, without ostentation; strictly economical without meanness; conscientiously pious without bigotry or intolerance; mild in his temper, meek and gentle in his demeanor, he kept his eye steadily fixed on his Divine Master, and in perfect humility of spirit endeavored as far as human nature permits, to tread in his steps.

Alfred Matthews was the youngest son of a younger branch of an honorable but reduced family, he received his early education at Eton, on the foundation, from whence he removed to Cambridge, where he finished his studies, and received the honors of the university; his moral character, steady deportment, and literary abilities had raised him so high in the esteem of the heads of the college, that he was recommended as private tutor, and afterwards became the travelling companion to the young Earl of Hartford and his brother, Lord John Milcombe. Returning from this tour, he for a considerable time became stationary as domestic chaplain in the family of the Earl. This nobleman had two sisters, the children of his mother by a former marriage, both by several years his seniors. The elder, Philippa, was of a serious cast, accomplished, sensible, well informed, pleasing in her person, and engaging in her manners. Constantia, the younger of the two, had been celebrated for her beauty, she was stately, somewhat affected, and very dictatorial: they were both highly tinctured with family pride, thinking the name of Cavendish, might rank almost with royalty itself; but withal so strongly attached to each other, that whatever one resolved to do or say, the other upheld as unquestionably right.

To both these ladies Mr. Matthews was an acceptable companion, and from the society of both he reaped the most unaffected pleasure.

He admired their talents, and esteemed their virtues; but his heart felt no warmer sentiment, till from several concurring circumstances, he could no but perceive, that the amiable Philippa evinced a tenderer attachment than her sister. On some subjects she could never converse with him without hesitation and blushes, while Constantia was easy and unembarrassed upon all topics. This discovery awakened his gratitude, but honor told him that the sister of his patron was in too elevated a station for him to hope to obtain her brother's consent to their union, he therefore requested permission to retire from the family.

"I am sorry to lose you from our family circle Mr. Matthews," said the Earl, when he mentioned his desire; "but it is natural that you should wish to have a fire-side of your own, and it is probable that you may also wish for a companion to make that fire-side cheerful, I must beg you so accept the Rectory of L—— which has lately become vacant and is in my gift, till something better can be offered." Every thing being arranged for his leaving the family, it was mentioned the next evening at supper. Philippa felt her color vary, but she neither looked up nor spoke; Constantia, turning towards him, with vivacity, inquired "How long he had taken the whim of keeping bachelor's hall, though I beg your pardon for the suggestion," said she, "perhaps some fair lady"—here she stopped, for Philippa's agitation was evident, and Constantia perceived that her brother noticed it.

When the ladies had retired, the Earl suddenly addressed his friend, "If I am not very much mistaken, Mr. Matthews, one of my sisters would have no objection to break in upon your bachelor scheme. Come, be candid, is the inclination mutual!" "I hope, my lord," replied Mr. Matthews, "that you do not suspect me of the presumption." "I see no presumption in it my friend," rejoined the Earl; "your family, your education, your talents, set you upon an equality with any woman, and though Philippa is not rich, yet her fortune and your income from the Rectory will supply the comforts, conveniences, and many of the elegances of life."

The conversation continued till the hour of repose, when after taking counsel of his pillow, Mr. Matthews resolved to solicit the favor of Miss Cavendish, and proved a successful wooer—a few months after, he became master of the Rectory—had a fire-side of his own, and an amiable companion to render that fire-side cheerful.

In the course of twenty years many changes had taken place: the Earl of Hartford had married a beautiful, but very dissipated woman, who, though she brought him but a very small fortune, knew extremely well how to make use of his, and diffuse its benefits in a most elegant and fashionable style. Her profusions knew no bounds, and, the Earl being taken off by a rapid fever, his affairs were found in so embarrassed a state that his sisters' fortunes, which had never been paid, though they had regularly received the interest, were reduced to less than one half their original value, which was twenty thousand pounds. With this comparatively small portion, Mrs. Matthews, and Mrs. Constantia Cavendish were obliged to be content.

Mr. Matthews continued Rector of L——, but no change of circumstances could lead him to accept a plurality of livings. It was a point of conscience with him to be paid for no more duty than he was able to perform himself, and as he was not able to allow a curate a liberal stipend, he employed none. When Mrs. Constantia argued with him on the subject; as she sometimes would; and wondered that he would perform all offices of the Rectorship himself, when he might have a curate who would think himself well paid by fifty pounds a year, and who would take the most troublesome part upon himself. "I should be sorry sister," he would reply "to consider any part of my duty a trouble, and what right have I to expect another to do for fifty pounds, what I am paid five hundred for doing? Every clergyman is, or should be a gentleman, and I think it highly disgraceful for one minister of the gospel to be lolling on velvet cushions, rolling in his carriage, and faring sumptuously everyday, while many, very many of his poor brethren, laborers in the same vineyard, bowed with poverty, burthened with large families, would, like Lazarus, be glad to feed on the crumbs that fall from the rich man's table."

But Mr. Matthews was an old fashioned person, and perhaps will not be thought very entertaining, so I will bring forward the young ladies.

III

The Three Orphans

We have already announced Lucy Blakeney, and if what has been said, does not give a competent idea of her character, we must leave it to time to develope; as to her person, it was of the middle size, perfectly well proportioned, and her figure and limbs had that roundness, which, in the eye of an artist, constitutes beauty. Her complexion was rather fair than dark, her eyes open, large, full hazel, her hair light brown, and her face animated with the glow of health and the smile of good humor.

Lady Mary Lumly had lost her mother a few years previous to the commencement of our story. She was an only child and had been indulged to a degree of criminality by this doatingly fond but weak mother, so that she had reached her sixteenth year without having had one idea impressed upon either head or heart that could in the least qualify her for rational society, or indeed for any society, but such as her fancy had created, from an indiscriminate perusal of every work of fiction that issued from the press. Her father died when she was an infant; his estates which had never been adequate to his expenses, passed with the title to a male branch of the family, her mother retired to her jointure house in Lancashire. Ill health secluded her from company, and finding her dear Mary averse from study, she sought in a governess for her daughter, more an easy companion for herself, than a conscientious able instructress for her child. The common elements of education, reading, writing, and English grammar, a little dancing, a little music, and a trifling knowledge of the French language constituted the whole of her accomplishments; when at the death of her mother, the guardian to whom the care of her little fortune had been intrusted, entreated Mrs. Matthews to receive her into her family. There was some relationship in the case, and Mrs. Cavendish thinking that with her romantic ideas, and uninformed mind, a boarding school, such as her income could afford, would not be a proper assylum for her, prevailed on her sister to accede to the proposal.

When scarcely past the age of childhood or indeed infancy, she had been allowed to sit beside her mother, while the tale of misfortune, of love or folly, was read aloud by the governess, and being possessed of a quick apprehension, strong sensibility, and a fertile imagination, she peopled the world, to which she was in effect a stranger, with lords and ladies, distressed beauties, and adoring lovers, to the absolute exclusion of every natural character, every rational idea, and truly moral or christian like feeling. Wealth and titles, which were sure to be heaped on the hero or heroine of the tale at last, she considered as the *ultimatum* of all sublunary good. Her mother had been a woman of high rank, but small fortune; she had therefore amongst other weak prejudices imbibed a strong predilection in favor of ancient nobility, and not to have a particle of noble blood flowing through one's veins was, in her opinion, to be quite insignificant.

This orphan of quality was as handsome as flaxen hair, light eyebrows, fair skin, blooming cheeks, and large glossy blue eyes could make her. The features of her face were perfectly regular but there was no expression in them, her smile was the smile of innocence, but it was also the smile of vacancy. She was tall, her limbs were long and her figure flat and lean; yet she thought herself a perfect model for a statuary. Her temper was naturally good, but the overweening pride and morbid sensibility, which were the fruits of the imprudent system of her education, rendered her quick to take offence where no offence was meant, and not unfrequently bathed her in tears, without any real cause. At the period when we introduced her to our readers, she was nearly seventeen years old, and had been under the care of Mr. Matthews, for the last four years.

Aura Melville completed the trio of fair orphans. Aura was the only child of a poor clergyman to whom Mr. Matthews had been, during a long and painful illness, an undeviating friend; she was ten years old, when death released her father from a state of suffering—her mother had been dead several years previous to this event.

It was an evening towards the end of July, the pale light of a moon just entered on its second quarter shone faintly into the chamber of the feeble invalid, a chamber to which he had been confined for more than eight months; the casement was open and the evening breeze passing through the blooming jessamine, that climbed the thatch of the humble cottage, wafted its refreshing perfume to cool the hectic cheek of the almost expiring Melville. He was seated in an easy chair, Mr. Matthews by his side, and the little Aura on a cushion at his feet, "Look, my own papa," said she, "how beautifully the moon shines; does not this cool breeze make you feel better? I love to look at the moon when it is new," continued she, "I do not know why, but it makes me feel so pleasantly, and yet sometimes I feel as if I could cry; and I say to myself what a good God our God is, to give us such a beautiful light to make our nights pleasant and cheerful, that, without it, are so dark and gloomy. Oh! my own dear papa, if it would but please our good God to make you well!" Melville pressed her hand, Mr. Matthews felt the drop of sensibility rise to his eye; but neither of them spoke.

The child, finding both remain silent, continued. "I hope you will be better, a great deal better, before next new moon." "I shall be well, quite well, my darling, in a very little time, said her father, for before this moon is at the full, I shall be at rest." "You will rest a good deal before that, I hope," said she with tender simplicity, then pausing a moment, she sprang up, and throwing her arms round his neck, she exclaimed, "Ah! I understand you now: Oh, my own dear papa! what will become of Aura! Oh, my good God, if it please you to let me die with my papa! for when he is gone there will be no one to love or care for his poor Aura." Her sobs impeded farther utterance—Melville had clasped the interesting child in his arms, his head sunk on her shoulder, her cheek rested on his. Mr. Matthews, fearing this tender scene would be too much for his debilitated frame, went towards them and endeavored to withdraw her from his embrace. At the slightest effort, his arms relaxed their hold, his head was raised from her shoulder, but instantly falling back against the chair, Mr. Matthews, shocked to the very soul, perceived that Aura was an orphan.

The poor child's anguish, when she discovered the truth, is not to be described. "She shall never want a protector," said he mentally, as he was leading her from the house of death to his own mansion.

"Philippa," said he, presenting Aura to his wife, "Providence has sent us a daughter; be a mother to her my dear companion, love her, correct her, teach her to be like yourself, she will then be most estimable."

Mrs. Matthews with all her family pride, possessed a kind and feeling heart, that heart loved most tenderly Alfred Matthews,—could she do otherwise than comply with his request? She took the poor girl to her bosom, and though she experienced not the most tender affection, yet Aura Melville found in her all the care and solicitude of a mother.

Her father had laid a good foundation in her innocent mind, and Mr. Matthews carefully completed the education he had begun, and at the age of nineteen, the period when first she appears in our pages, she was a pleasing well informed young woman; highly polished in her manners, yet without one showy accomplishment. She knew enough of music to enjoy and understand its simple beauties, but she performed on no instrument. She moved gracefully, and could, if called upon, join a cotillion or contra dance, without distressing others; her understanding was of the highest order, and so well cultivated that she could converse with sense and propriety on almost any subject. Yet unobtrusive, modest and humble, she was silent and retired, unless called forth by the voice of kindness and encouragement. She was beloved in the family; industrious, discreet, cheerful, good humored, grateful to her benefactors, and contented with her lot; she won the regard and without exacting it, gained the respect of all who knew her.

IV

Romance, Piety, Sensibility

Lucy, after the gentle reproof she received from Mr. Matthews, was careful not to go out in the evening without a companion; she frequently visited the cottages of the poor class of industrious peasants, and as her allowance for clothes and pocket money was liberal and her habits by no means expensive, she had many opportunities of relieving the distresses of some, and adding to the comforts of others. Sometimes she would tempt lady Mary to ramble with her, but that young lady but little understood the common incidents, and necessities of life, and even had she comprehended them ever so well, she was so thoughtless in her expenditure on dress and trifles, that she seldom had anything to bestow. Aura Melville was therefore her usual associate and adviser in these visits of charity. Her bosom sympathized in their sufferings, and her judgment suggested the relief likely to be of most benefit.

One evening lady Mary had been walking with a young lady in the neighborhood, whose tastes and feelings resembled her own, when, just as the family where preparing to take their tea, she rushed into the parlor and in a flood of tears exclaimed, "Oh, my dear sir, my kind Mr. Matthews, if you do not help me I shall lose my senses." "How, my dear?" said he, approaching the seat on which she had thrown herself in an attitude of the utmost distress. "Oh, sir," said she, sobbing, "I must have five guineas directly, for I wanted so many things when you paid me my last quarter's allowance, that I have not a guinea left." "I am sorry for that," replied Mr. Matthews, "for you know that it will be six weeks before another payment is due." "Oh yes, I know that: but I thought you would be so good as to lend it to me on this very, very urgent occasion!" "And pray what may the very, very urgent occasion be?" asked he smiling, and placing a chair near the tea-table, he motioned with his hand for her to draw nigh and partake the social meal, for which the rest of the family were now waiting.

"I cannot eat, indeed I cannot, sir," she replied with an hysterical sob, "I can do nothing till you comply with my request."

"That I certainly shall not do at present, child. I must understand for what this sum is required, and how you mean to dispose of it. Five guineas, lady Mary, is a considerable sum; it should not be hastily or unadvisedly lavished away. It might rescue many suffering individuals from absolute want."

"Yes, sir, it is for that I want it, I know you will let me have it." "I, am not quite so sure about that. But come, Mary Lumly," for so the good man was wont to call her when he was pleased with her, "come, draw nigh and take your tea, after which you shall tell your story and tomorrow morning we will see what can be done."

"Tomorrow! sir, tomorrow!" exclaimed she wildly, "tomorrow, it may be too late, they are suffering the extremity of want, and are you so cold hearted as to talk of tomorrow?"

Miss Blakeney and Aura Melville exchanged looks with each other. Mr. Matthews sat down and began his tea. "You must permit me to tell you, lady Mary Lumly," said Mrs. Cavendish, in her stately manner, "that this is very unbecoming behaviour, you call it no doubt sensibility; but you give it too dignified a name. It is an affectation of fine feeling, it arises more from a wish to display your own humanity, than from any genuine sympathy. The heart has little to do with it. You have spoken rudely to my brother Matthews; he, worthy man, knows what true sensibility is, and is actuated by its dictates, though you, disrespectful girl, have called him cold hearted."

Resentment at being spoken to, in so plain a style, soon dried lady Mary's tears. She seated herself at the tea table, took her cup, played with her spoon, poured the tea into the saucer, then back into the cup; in short, did everything but drink it.

The tea service removed, Mr. Matthews said, "come hither, Mary Lumly, and now let us hear your tragical tale." Lady Mary's excessive enthusiasm had by this time considerably abated, but she felt somewhat vexed at the plain, well meant reproof of Mrs. Cavendish. However, she seated herself on the sofa beside Mr. Matthews, and in a conciliatory tone began. "I am afraid that I have not been so respectful as I ought to be, sir, but my feelings ran away with me." "Your impetuosity, you should say, child," interrupted Mrs. Cavendish. Lady Mary colored highly. "The evening is really very fine," said the good Rector, "come, Mary, you and I will go and inhale the sweets of the flowers," then drawing her arm under his, he led her into the garden.

"So you have been taking a ramble with Miss Brenton this afternoon."

"Yes, sir, and we went farther than we intended, for we went through the little copse, and took a path which neither of us had any knowledge of, and having walked a considerable way without seeing any house, or meeting anyone, we began to feel alarmed." "I think you were very imprudent, Mary, you might have encountered ill bred clowns or evil minded persons who would have insulted you."

"I know it, sir, but I am very glad I went, for all that."

"How so?"

"Why, just as we began to feel a little frightened, we heard a child cry, and following the sound, we came to a very wretched hovel, for it could not be called even a cottage. At the door sat a child about four years old crying. 'What is the matter child?' said Miss Brenton. 'Mammy is sick and granny fell out of her chair, and daddy a'n't come home yet.' We both of us were in the hut in a moment, Oh! dear sir, I never shall forget it, on the bed as they called it, but it was only some straw laid upon a kind of shelf made of boards and covered with a ragged blanket, so dirty that I was almost afraid to go near it, and—and—on this wretched bed lay a poor pale woman with a little, very little baby on her arm."

Lady Mary's lip quivered, Mr. Matthews pressed her hand and said, "But the poor old granny? you have not told me about her."

"She had been up all the preceding night with her daughter, and not having any help all day, or much nourishment I believe, she had fainted and fell out of her chair; the little girl whose crying had brought us to the place, had run out in great alarm; but when we entered the house, the old woman had recovered, and was sitting, pale as a ghost and unable to articulate, by the handful of fire, over which hung an iron pot,"

"Why this is a most deplorable tale, my dear Mary."

"But I have not told you the worst, sir."

"Why I suppose the worst was, you had no money to give them?"

"No I had a crown in my purse, and I gave it to the old woman, who as she looked at it burst into tears and recovering her speech, said, 'God forever bless you.'"

"But had Miss Brenton nothing to give?"

"Oh no, sir, she said her sensibility was so great she could not stay in the hovel, and they were so dirty that she was afraid of contracting some infectious disorder."

"Then that was the worst, for I suppose she ran away and left you?"

"Yes she did, and said she would wait for me by the road side, so while I was inquiring what they most wanted, and the poor sick woman with the baby, said, 'everything,' a rough looking man with two boys and a girl came in; he went to the sick woman, asked her how she did, and then turning to the old woman said, 'Mother, is there anything for supper?' 'Yes, thank God,' said the mother, 'I have got summut for ye, John, which a kind hearted christian man gave me this morn.' She then opened the pot, took out a small piece of meat, and two or three turnips, and said, 'there, John, is a nice piece of mutton, and Sally has supped a little of the broth, oh! 'twas a great comfort to her, and here, dears, taking up some of the water in which the meat had been boiled, in poringers, here's a nice supper for ye all.' She then gave the children each a piece of bread, so black, that I ran out of the place ashamed that my curiosity had kept me there so long, when I had so little to give."

"It was not curiosity, Mary, it was a better feeling: but had you been mistress of five guineas, and had them in your purse at that moment would you have given them?"

"Oh yes, ten, if I could have commanded them, but now, sir, that you know the whole, you will, I am sure, lend me the money."

"We will see about it tomorrow, your crown will for the present provide a few necessaries, so rest in quiet, my good girl, for believe me the bit of boiled mutton and turnips were heartily relished by the man; and the water as you call it, the children, who I suppose had been out at work all day, ate with a keener appetite than you would have partaken of the most delicate viands."

The next morning lady Mary, who was not an early riser, and did not generally make her appearance till the rest of the family were seated at the breakfast table, was surprised, upon entering the parlor, to find Miss Blakeney, and Miss Melville had just returned from a walk in which they had been accompanied by their guardian, their hair disordered by the morning breeze and their countenances glowing with health and pleasure.

"You are an idler, Mary Lumly," said Mr, Matthews, "but exercise is so necessary to preserve health that I am resolved that you shall accompany me in a round of visits to some of my parishioners this morning." This was an invitation he frequently gave to one or the other of the fair orphans under his protection. The morning was fine, and lady Mary hoping he would take the path through the copse, readily assented, and being soon equipped for her walk, gaily tripped by his side till she found that he took a directly opposite path to what she had expected.

"I was in hopes you would have gone with me to visit the poor people I mentioned," said she in rather a supplicating voice. "All in good time, child," he replied, "I have several poor and sick persons to visit." The first cottage they entered, they saw a pale looking woman at her spinning; near her, two children seated on a stool held a spelling book between them, and in an old high backed arm chair sat a man, the very picture of misery; his feet and hands were wrapped in coarse flannel. Every thing around them indicated extreme poverty, yet everything was perfectly clean: the children's clothes were coarse, but not ragged, the mother preferring a patch of a different color, to a hole or rent.

"How are you, neighbor?" said Mr. Matthews, "and how are you, my good dame, and how do you contrive to keep all so tight and orderly, when you have a sick husband to attend, and nothing but your own labor to support him, yourself and your children?"

"Oh, sir," said the woman, rising, "we have much to be thankful for. The good Sir Robert Ainslie has ordered his steward to let us live in this cottage, rent free, till my husband shall get better, and the house keeper lets little Bessey here a pitcher of milk and a plate of cold meat every now and then, so, please your reverence, we are not so bad off as we might be."

"What is the matter with your husband?" asked lady Mary, with a look of wonder at the woman's expression of contentment, when there was so much apparent wretchedness around her.

"Why, your ladyship, Thomas, though he be an industrious kind husband, was never over strong; he worked too hard, and last summer took a bad fever; and when he was getting better he would go to work again before he had got up his strength; the season was very wet and he was out late and early, so, you see, he got a bad cold, and his fever came on worse than ever, and the rheumatics set in, and ever since he has been a cripple like, not being able to use his hands or feet."

"Dear me, that is very terrible," said lady Mary, "how can you possibly live, how do you get time to work?"

"I gets up early, my lady, and sits up late; sometimes I can earn, one way or another, three and sixpence a week, and sometimes, but not very often, five shillings."

"Five shillings!" repeated the astonished Mary, "can four people live on five shillings a week?"

Mr. Matthews had been, during this time, talking with the invalid, but catching her last words he replied,

"Aye, child, and many worthy honest christians with larger families are obliged to do with less."

"We, I am sure," said Thomas, "ought not to complain, thanks be to God and my good dame, we are main comfortable, but I fear me, your

SUSANNA ROWSON

reverence, she will kill herself, she washes and mends our clothes when she ought to be resting, after spinning all day or going out to work, to help the gentlefolks' servants to wash and clean house. I sometimes hope and pray that I may soon recover the use of my hands and feet, or that it will please my Maker to lay me at rest."

"No! no! heaven forbid, Thomas, I can work very well, I can be content with anything, so you are spared, and you will get well by and by, and then we shall all be happy again."

The tears which had for sometime trembled in lady Mary's eyes, now rushed down her cheeks, she drew forth her empty purse and looked beseechingly at Mr. Matthews. He did not particularly notice her, but asked, "Does the doctor attend you regularly? Is he kind and considerate?"

"Oh yes, sir, and we gets all the physic and such stuff from the Potticary without paying, thanks to you reverend, sir, then the housekeeper at the great house sent us some oatmeal and sago, a nutmeg and a whole bottle of wine, and that has made poor Thomas comfortable for above a month past. Oh we have so many blessings."

Mr. Matthews gave the woman an approving smile, and presenting her with half a crown, said, "This young lady desires me to give you this, it may enable you to add a little to your comforts. Good morning, continue this humble contented frame of mind, and rely on your heavenly Father, he will in his own good time relieve you from your difficulties, or enable you to support them with patience."

"My dear sir," said lady Mary when they had lef the cottage, "what a trifle you gave to that distressed family."

"Mary," replied the Rector, "it is not the bestowing large sums that constitutes real benevolence, nor do such donations ultimately benefit the persons on whom they are bestowed, they rather serve to paralyze the hand of industry, while they lead the individual to depend on adventitious circumstances for relief, instead of exerting his own energies to soften or surmount the difficulties with which he may be surrounded."

Many other calls were made in the course of the morning, till at length they stopped at a very small cottage, and on entering, Mary was struck with the appearance of an elderly man and woman both seemingly past the period of being useful either to themselves or others. A few embers were in the grate, over which hung a teakettle, and on a deal table stood a pewter teapot, some yellow cups and saucers and a piece of the same kind of bread, the sight of which had filled her with disgust the evening before, a little dark brown sugar and about a gill of skimmed milk completed the preparation for their humble meal.

"Why you are early at your tea, or late at your breakfast, Gammer," said Mr. Matthews as he entered. The old dame laid down the patchwork with which she had been employing herself, and her husband closed the bible in which he was reading.

"Bless you, good sir," said he, "tea is often all our sustenance and serves for breakfast, dinner and supper, but we are old, and can take but little exercise, so a little food suffices; if sometimes we can get a morsel of bacon or a crumb of cheese to relish our bread, it is quite a treat, and a herring laid on the coals is a feast indeed; but it is long since we have known better times, and we be got used to the change. I wish indeed sometimes that I had something to comfort my poor old dame, but since the death of our little darlings, what sustains our tottering frames is of little consequence; we are thankful for what we have."

"Thankful," said lady Mary internally, "thankful for such a poor shed to keep them from the weather, such a miserable looking bed to rest their old limbs upon, and some black tea and dry bread for their only meal."

Mr. Matthews saw that she was struck, and willing to give her time for rumination sat down beside the old man on a stool. The only vacant wooden chair being dusted by the dame, lady Mary seated herself and pursuing her train of thought, audibly said, "I should think, poor woman, you had cause for repining and discontent rather than thankfulness."

"Ah no lady," she replied, "what right have I to expect more than others; how many thousands in this kingdom have not even a hovel to shelter them, scarcely a rag to cover them, and only the bare ground to sleep on, whilst their poor children beg their daily bread from door to door."

"Dreadful!" said lady Mary, and her cheek assumed a marble hue.

"But that is not the worst," continued the woman, "many of these poor souls are as ignorant as the black-amoors of Africa, they cannot read their bibles; they do not know that idleness is next to thieving; they do not know the God who made them, or the Saviour who redeemed them. How much happier are we! This is a poor place to be sure, but it is our own, and if our bed is hard, we can lie down with quiet consciences; if we have but little food we eat it with thankfulness; and when we are low spirited, our frames feeble and our hearts oppressed, we can read the word of consolation in God's own book. Oh lady, these are great blessings."

SUSANNA ROWSON

"But I understood from what your husband said, that you had seen better days; how can you bring your mind to bear the ills of age and poverty without complaint."

"It is because I know that He who has allotted my portion knows what is best for me. It is because I am fully sensible that his bounties are far beyond my deserts."

"What? such poor fare! such a hut! and you a good well conducted woman, and these wretched accommodations more than you deserve?"

"Yes, lady, had the best of us no more than we deserve, our portion would be hard indeed. You say I have seen better days, so I have. But I weary you, and I beg your pardon too, reverend sir."

"You have it, dame, go on, tell your story to that young lady, I have much to say to your good man."

Thus encouraged, Gammer Lounsdale again addressed her attentive auditor. "When I married my good man there, I had three hundred pounds, which had been left me by my grandfather, and my husband had scraped together about as much more. So we stocked a farm, and for years went on quite well; we never had but one child, it was a girl, and, God forgive us! we were very proud of her, for Alice Lonsdale grew up a very pretty young woman. I taught her to be domestic, and to use her needle, but alack-a-day, I did not teach her to know herself. There was our first great fault, and when the people praised her beauty or her singing, (for Alice sung sweetly lady,) we used to join in the praise, and her father, poor man, would chuck her under the chin, and say aye! aye! in good time we shall see our girl either a 'squire's or a parson's lady. So Alice grew vain and conceited, and in an evil hour we consented that she should pay a visit to a neighboring market town, and attend a dancing school, for as we had settled it in our weak heads that she was to be a lady, it was but right that she should learn to dance.

"Alice was now turned of fifteen, and during the time of her visit to Dorking, (for at that period we lived in Surry,) she became acquainted with a young man, the son of a reputable tradesman in that town. After her return, he sometimes called to see her, and, to make short of my story, when she was eighteen, with the consent of both his parents and her own, Alice became his wife. We gave her five hundred pounds, his father gave him seven hundred, which furnished a small house neatly in Croyden, where he had some family connections, and stocked a shop in the grocery line.

"For sometime things went on smoothly; and when her father and I visited them about a year after their marriage, we thought they were getting beforehand. He appeared to be industrious and attentive, and Alice was cheerful and happy. I staid with my poor girl during her first confinement, and was very proud of the little grandson with which she presented me. After this I saw her no more for two years, but I used to fancy that her letters were not so sprightly as formerly. However, I knew that when a woman becomes a wife and mother, the vivacity of girlhood is sobered. However some reports having reached us that her husband was become unsteady, and that it was thought he was much involved in debt, my good man took a journey to inquire about it. He found things worse than had been represented. Alice was pale, dejected and miserable; her husband had got acquainted with a set of worthless beings who called themselves honest fellows; frequented clubs, and acted private plays, which being done once in the hall of a public house and money taken for admission, they were all taken up and had to pay a heavy fine.

"My husband had not been many days in Croyden, before he had reason to think, that Alice was injured in the tenderest point, and that with her own domestic; but she made no complaint, and while her father was considering what he should do that might best promote her happiness, Lewis, for that was her husband's name, was arrested for fifteen hundred pounds, on his note which he had given for stock, and as we afterwards learnt, sold at under price to supply his extravagance. Alice pleaded with her father to assist him, her situation was delicate, and old Mr. Lewis being sent for, his affairs were compromised, the two fathers being bound for him.

"My good man then returned home, where he had not been more than a month, when one evening just at dusk, a chaise stopped at the gate, and in a few moments, Alice, leading her little boy, ran up the walk, and throwing herself into my arms with an hysterical seb fainted. It was long before she could articulate. At length she told us old Mr. Lewis was dead, his property was not sufficient to pay his debts, that her heartless husband had taken what valuables he could collect, and raised money upon everything that was not already mortgaged, and absconded with the abandoned woman I told you about. He had told Alice that he was going to Dorking to look into his late father's affairs. Ah, lady, he had been there before, and gleaned all he could from the wreck, even to the leaving his old widowed mother destitute. The same night the woman who lived with Alice, having asked leave to go out, never returned, and upon examination it was found that she had taken her clothes, to which she had added some of the most valuable belonging to her mistress.

"The next day the furniture of the house was taken by a man who said he had advanced money upon it, and my poor girl was literally turned into the street. In this distress the landlord of a large inn had compassion on her. He advanced her a few guineas and sent her in his own chaise to her father, her best and only friend.

"I found upon inquiry that my child had not been altogether faultless, she had been thoughtless in her expenses, and never having been controlled in her youth, she could not practice the necessary patience and forbearance which her situation required; so that instead of weaning her unhappy partner from his pursuits, she perhaps irritated his temper and made him more dissipated. A few days after her return, my husband was arrested upon the note, and being unable to pay so large a sum, his stock upon his farm was seized, and not being able to meet his rent, which from various circumstances had run for six months, we were obliged to quit the farm and take a cottage a little way from Croyden. Here Alice gave birth to a daughter and a few days after was laid at rest in the grave. But our misfortunes were not ended. Though by working hard and living poor, we kept free from debt, yet it was a struggle to maintain the two children.

"But we managed to keep them clean and tidy, so that they went to school, and lovely babies they were, and my vain proud heart made them my idols, but it was God's will that I should be humbled to the very dust. One night the thatch of our cottage caught fire and we awoke almost suffocated with smoke. We sprang up; I caught up the girl and ran out, but before my husband could escape with the boy, a rafter fell, and I thought I had lost them both, but with great struggling he got out, though greatly bruised and burnt. The child was so hurt that he was a cripple as long as he lived.

"We were now houseless, pennyless and naked; neither of us very young, my health not good, and my husband likely to be confined months before he could go to work, if indeed he should be ever able to work again. A cottager who lived about a mile from us, who had got up early to carry something to Croyden market, saw the fire, and calling his son, they ran to our assistance, but nothing was saved. He took my husband on his back; the lad took the boy; both father and son had pulled off their outer jackets to wrap them round me and my little girl; and we proceeded as well as we could to neighbor Woodstock's cottage.

"They did all they could for us, but they were poor themselves. However, on applying to the 'squire, of whom we had rented the hut, we had lived in, he bade his housekeeper send us some old clothes. She not only obeyed him in that, but brought us some little comforts, and with her came a sweet boy about the age of little Alice. When this dear child went back, he told his father, who was then visiting the 'squire, how poor and how sick we were, and the next day brought him to see us.

"Sir Robert Ainslie, for it was he himself, spoke to us kindly, gave us money to purchase some clothing, and procured a doctor to visit my husband and grandson; he also spoke to the minister about us, and he came to console and pray with us. Oh, lady, that was the greatest charity of all; for we did not know where to look for consolation till he taught us. We had never considered that a good and all wise Father has a right to chastise his children when and how he pleases; we had been full of complaining and discontent before. But he read to us and prayed with us, and at length convinced us that it was possible to be happy though poor.

"When my husband got able to move about, the dear boy, master Ainslie, came with his father, one day, and laying a folded paper on my lap said, 'Papa gives you that.' So I opened it and found it was a gift of this place we now live in, and a promise of five guineas a year as long as I lived.

"I could not speak to thank him. He told me that he had lately purchased an estate in Hampshire; that he had been to look at it and have it put in repair, just before he came into Surry; that he recollected this cottage, and had written to his steward to have it got ready for us, and that he would have us sent to it free of all expense.

"Well, in a short time we moved here and were happier than we had ever been in our lives before, for Sir Robert wrote about us to our good Rector here, who has comforted and strengthened our minds. Our dear Alice grew apace; she earned a little towards clothing herself, and then she was so dutiful to her grandfather and me, and so kind to her crippled brother! But seven years agone last Lammas, the small pox came into the neighborhood. The boy took it first. Nothing could separate his sister from him, and in one short week I followed both my darlings to the grave."

The old woman stopped a moment, put her hand to her forehead, then looking up meekly, cried in an under tone, "Thy will be done! It will not be long before I go to them, but they can never return to me. It was the hand of mercy that took them, for what had they to make life desirable. The boy's inheritance was decrepitude and poverty, and poor Alice had all her mother's beauty, and who knows what snares might have been laid, what temptations might have assailed her. She might have been lost both soul and body. Now, thanks be to God! she is safe in the house of her heavenly Father."

"Come, child, it is time for us to be walking," exclaimed Mr. Matthews, so taking leave of the old people, he led her out of the cottage. Perceiving her cheeks wet with tears which she was endeavoring to conceal, "These are good tears," said he, "indulge them freely, they flow from pity and admiration."

"From pity, indeed," she replied, "but I cannot admire what I do not rightly understand." Then pausing a moment, she continued, "Pray, sir, are not these people Methodists?"

"What do you mean by a Methodist?"

"I hardly know how to explain myself, but I know I have often heard my mamma and governess laugh about some folks that lived in our neighborhood, who used to talk a great deal about religion, and pray and sing psalms, even when they were in trouble, and they called them Methodists!"

"Is it then," said Mr. Matthews gravely, "a ridiculous thing to say our prayers, or praise the name of Him from whom all our blessings proceed?"

"No, sir, but when he has taken from us those we love, it is difficult to feel perfectly resigned. I am sure I could not praise him when my mamma died."

"But you could pray to him, I hope?"

"No, indeed I could not, I thought him very cruel."

"Poor child," said he tenderly, "what a barren waste thy mind was at that time."

"But you have made me better, sir."

"I hope God will make you wiser, my love! And now, Mary, let me advise you, never to use the term Methodist in this way again. Dame Lonsdale and her husband are good pious members of the church of England; they are what every christian should be, humble, devout, and grateful, but let the mode in which they worship, be what it may, if they are sincere, they will be accepted: there are many roads to the foot of the cross, and which ever may be taken, if it is pursued with a pure and upright heart, is safe, and He who suffered on it, will remove every burthen from us whether it be earthly affliction, or sorrow for committed offences." While Mr. Matthews was speaking, a sudden turn in the road made lady Mary start, for she beheld just before her, the identical cottage to which she had been so desirous to come when they first began their ramble.

V

A Lesson, Change of Scene

As I live, sir," said she in delight, "there is the place I wanted to visit." "Then we will go in and see how the poor people are," said Mr. Matthews.

They entered, but how changed was the scene, a clean though coarsely furnished bed stood in one corner of the room; the old, wooden frame had been removed; the room was neatly swept and sanded, a new sauce pan was by the fire, in which gruel was boiling, the sick woman and her infant were in clean clothes befitting their station, and the old mother also appeared in better habiliments whilst a healthy looking young woman was busied about some domestic concerns.

Every thing wore such a look of comfort, that lady Mary thought she had mistaken the place. But the old woman recognized her, and rising, began to say how lucky her good ladyship's visit had been to them all, for that morning two beautiful young ladies came to see them.

"Mayhap" continued she, "they be your sisters, though they were so good natured and condescending, they seemed more like angels than aught else; and it was not more than two hours after they went away before a man came to the door with a cart, and what should be in it, think ye, but that nice, bedstead and bed, with blankets, and sheets, and coverlet, and some clothes for Sally and her baby and he brought that good young body to tend she till she be up again; dear heart! how John will be surprised when he comes home, he won't know his place, not he, but will think the fairies have been hero.

"Ah!" said lady Mary, looking at Mr. Matthews, "I fancy I know who the fairies were."

The Rector put his finger on his lip, and telling the woman that he was glad to find they were so well provided for, he led his ward from the cottage.

"Now, Mary," said he smiling, "how much do you think those fairies whom you so shrewdly guess at, expended for all the comforts and conveniences, these poor people seem to have acquired, since last evening."

"Oh! a great deal," said she, "more than five guineas, I dare say. First there is a bed—"

"That is not a bed, but a second hand mattrass, which, though a good one, cost little or nothing. The blankets and coverlet, came from my house, and are with the bed linen *lent* only. If we find the woman on her recovery, industrious, clean, and well behaved, they will be given to her. The rest was very trifling, a little tea, oatmeal, sugar, and materials for brown bread, half a cheese, half a side of bacon, some coal and candles, were all purchased for less than a guinea and a half. Had you given the sum you intended, they would have squandered it away, and not made themselves half so comfortable. I make a point of inquiring the characters of any poor, who are my parishioners, before I give them any relief, and this morning while Lucy and Aura were visiting your proteges, I investigated their character. The man is an honest hard working fellow, his wife, I find from good authority, is idle, and by no means cleanly in her habits. You, child, have no idea how much the prosperity and comfort of a poor man, and often of a rich man too, depends on the conduct of his wife. The old woman is his wife's mother, she is old and feeble, can do but little, and often, by a querulous temper, makes things worse than they would otherwise be. You say the children were ragged and dirty; I shall see that they are comfortably clothed, and, if I find that the clothes are kept whole and clean, I will befriend the family farther, but if they are let run to rags, without washing or mending, I shall do no more."

Thus, in walking, chatting, making various calls and commenting on the scenes they witnessed, time passed unobserved by lady Mary. At length Mr. Matthews, drawing out his watch, exclaimed, "I protest, it is almost four o'clock."

"Indeed!" said Mary, "I am afraid we shall have dinner waiting." The Rector's hour of dining was half past three.

"I do not think they will wait," he replied, "I have frequently requested they would not wait for me, for you know I am frequently detained by a sick bed, or an unhappy person whose mind is depressed."

They had now a mile to walk, and lady Mary assured the Rector that she was "very, very hungry!" Arriving at home they discovered that the family had dined, and the ladies gone out on some particular purpose. A cloth had been therefore laid in the study for the ramblers.

"Come," said Mr. Matthews, "sit down, Mary, you say you are hungry, we will waive ceremony on this occasion, and you shall dine in your morning dress.

"What have we here?" he continued raising a cover, and discovering part of a boiled leg of mutton, which had been kept perfectly hot, and on a dish beside it stood a few turnips not mashed.

"Are there no capers John?"

"No sir, the cook did not recollect that they were out till it was too late to get any, and my mistress said she was sure you would excuse it."

"Well, well, we must do as well as we can," said he, laying a slice of mutton and one of the turnips, on lady Mary's plate.

She did not wait for other sauce than a keen appetite, but having dispatched two or three slices of the meat, with a good quantity of the vegetable and bread, declared she never had relished a dinner so well in her life.

"You will have a bit of tart?" said the Rector, "I warrant John can find one or bit of cheese and biscuit."

"Oh no! my dear sir, I have eaten so heartily."

"Poor dear young woman!" said Mr. Matthews, in an affected tone of sensibility, "how my heart aches for you, out all the morning, walking from cottage to cottage, coming home hungry and weary, and had nothing to eat but a bit of boiled mutton and turnips, and to wash it down, a glass of cold water." Here Mr. Matthews pretended to sob; when lady Mary comprehending the ridicule, burst out a laughing.

"You see, my child," said he, assuming his own kind and gracious manner, "how misplaced sensibility is, when it fancies anything more than wholesome fare, however plain or course it may be, is necessary to satisfy the appetite of those whom exercise or labor have rendered really hungry. Where indeed there is a scanty quantity, it should awaken our good feelings, and lead us to extend the hand of charity."

"Dear sir," said lady Mary, "you have this day taught me a lesson that I trust through life I shall never forget."

Month after month, and year after year, passed on while Mr. Matthews was endeavoring to cultivate the understandings, fortify the principles, and, by air and exercise, invigorate the frames of his fair wards. During the six pleasantest months, masters in music and drawing, from Southampton, attended lady Mary and Miss Blakeney, and the other six, they employed themselves in imparting what they had gained to Aura Melville, in her leisure hours.

Thus they were improved in a far greater degree, by the attention necessary to bestow on every acquirement in which they were desirous to instruct her. There were many genteel families in the neighborhood, but none visited on a more intimate footing, than that of Sir Robert Ainslie. His son Edward, had become a great favorite at the Rectory, ever since they had known the story of old dame Lonsdale and the cottage; but as he was pursuing his studies at Oxford, they saw him but seldom.

It was in the summer of 1794, when Lucy had just entered her twentieth year, that Mrs. Cavendish proposed that, to change the scene, and give the young people a glimpse of the fashionable world, a few weeks should be spent in Brighton, and that, the ensuing winter, they should go to London. Mr. and Mrs. Matthews were fondly attached to the place where they had passed so many happy years, yet, sensible that Lucy in particular, should be introduced properly into a world where she would most likely be called upon to act a prominent part, they consented, and about the latter part of June, they commenced their journey.

Sir Robert Ainslie and his son were to meet them there, for Edward was to be their escort to public places, when Mr. Matthews felt disinclined to mix in the gay scenes of fashionoble life, their attendant in the walks upon the Stiene, or excursions in the beautiful environs of Brighton.

This was very pleasant to the whole party. The elderly ladies were fond of the society of Sir Robert. Mr. Matthews regarded him as an old and esteemed friend, and the young ones as a kind of parent, and his son as their brother. Lady Mary, indeed, could have fancied herself in love with Edward, and often in the most pathetic terms lamented to her young companions that he was not *nobly born*, he was so handsome, so generous, so gallant.

"Yes," said Aura, with an arch glance from under her long eyelashes, "so generally gallant that no one can have the vanity to suppose herself a particular favorite."

"No, indeed that is true, and I should lament to find *myself* particularized by him, as you know my poor mother used to say, she should not rest in her grave if she thought I should ever match myself with anyone below the rank of nobility."

"I think," said Aura, laughing, "you need be under no apprehension, unless indeed it should be from the fear that should he offer, you might not be able to keep your resolution."

They were soon settled in their new abode at Brighton, their names enrolled on the books at the rooms, libraries, &c. and the unaffected manners of the three fair orphans, their simple style of dress, unobtrusive beauty, and the general report that they were all three heiresses, drew numerous admirers and pretenders, around them. But the grave and gentlemanly manners of Mr. Matthews, the stately hauteur of Mrs. Cavendish, with the brotherly attention of Edward Ainslie, kept impertinence and intrusion at an awful distance.

Edward felt kindly to all, but his heart gave the preference to Lucy, though he feared to give way to its natural impulse, lest the world, nay, even the object of his tenderness, should think him interested.

Sir Robert Ainslie had two sons and a daughter by a former marriage; these were married and settled, and were too much the seniors of the present young party to ever have been in habits of intimacy with them. The mother of Edward had survived his birth but a few years; and he became the consoler, delight, and darling of his father. The youth was endowed with fine talents, a mind of the strictest rectitude, and perhaps a remark that his cool, calculating, eldest brother once made, that it would be a fine *spec* for Ned, if he could catch the handsome heiress, led him to put a curb on that sensibility and admiration, which might otherwise have led him to appear as her professed lover.

One fine morning, as they were strolling on the Stiene, an elegant youth, in military uniform, accosted him with "Ainslie, my dear lad, how are you, this is a lucky encounter for me, for I hope you spend sometime here, my regiment is here on duty for six months." Edward received his proffered hand with great cordiality, and presenting him to the ladies as lieutenant Franklin, of the—regiment, named to his friend, each of the fair trio, and he joining the party, they sauntered on the sands an hour longer, waited on the ladies to Mr. Matthews' door, and then both gentlemen bade them good morning.

"Why, you are in luck's way, Ned," said the officer, "to be on such easy terms with the graces, for really I must say your three beauties are worthy that appellation. Are you in anyway related to either of them?"

"By no means," he replied, "my father is guardian to one, who is a splendid heiress, and in habits of great intimacy with the reverend Mr. Matthews, who is guardian to the other two."

"Heiresses also, eh! Ned?"

"Not exactly so, one has a genteel independence, the other, poor girl, is an orphan, whose family is only known to her guardian, and whose fortune, if report says true, depends entirely on his kindness."

"But which is the heiress?"

"That I shall leave to your sagacity to discover, but I hope you do not mean to set out in life, with interested views in the choice of a partner?"

"Oh no, my good grandfather took care I should have no occasion to do that, he left me enough for comfort, and even elegance, with prudent management, and as I have no propensities for gaming, racing, or other fashionable follies, I shall look out for good nature, good sense, and dirscretion in a wife, in preference to wealth. To be sure, a little beauty, and a handsome address, would, though not indispensable, be very acceptable qualities."

Lieutenant Franklin was the eldest of four sons, his father was an officer of artillery, had seen some hard service, passed a number of years abroad, and during that period had accumulated a large fortune. He had married the only daughter of a wealthy man, resident in the part of the world where he was stationed; was intrusted by government with providing military stores, &c. during a seven years' war, for a large army in actual service, and when the war was ended, returned to his own country; which he had left nine years before, a captain of artillery, with little besides his pay, an honorable descent, and fair character, to receive the thanks of royalty for his intrepidity, and to dash into the world of splendor and gaiety. His house was one of the most elegant in Portland place, his equipage and establishment, such as might have become a nobleman of the first rank. Bellevue, a large estate near Feversham in Kent, consisting of a large handsome and commodious mansion, several well tenanted farms, pleasure grounds, fish ponds, green and hot houses, was purchased for his summer residence.

Promoted to the rank of colonel of artillery, and having held the office of chief engineer during his service abroad, the father of lieutenant Franklin stood in an elevated rank, bad associated with the first personages in the kingdom. His eldest son, as has been mentioned, was amply provided for, and had chosen the army for his profession. The others, as yet little more than boys, were finishing their education at some of the best establishments near London. His two daughters, Julia and Harriet, were attended by masters at home, under the superintendence of an excellent governess.

From the moment of his introduction to the family of Mr. Matthews, Sir Robert Ainslie having spoken of him in high terms, Mr. Franklin became a frequent and always a welcome guest. Though Miss Blakeney was known to have an independent fortune, its extent was not confined even to herself; for Mr. Matthews knew that wealth attracts flattery, and good as he believed Lucy's heart to be, he feared for the frailty of human nature, if exposed to the breath of that worst of mental poisons, injudicious and indiscriminate adulation.

A cursory observer would never have taken Lucy for the independent heiress, the retired modesty of her manners, the respectful deference which she paid her guardian and his family, united to an intuitive politeness and real affection with which she ever distinguished Aura Melville, would have led anyone to think she was the dependent.

Lady Mary was afraid of Aura, her wit, though in general harmlessly playful, was sometimes sarcastic, and the vain girl of quality often smarted under its lash, and if she met the steady eye of Aura, at a time when she was displaying airs of self complacency, her own would sink under it. The seniors of the family encouraged this involuntary respect paid to their protegee, and by their own manner towards her gave their visitors reason to think, that they were receiving, rather than conferring a favor, by her residence among them.

Thus every circumstance coincided to establish the general idea entertained that Aura was the independent heiress, lady Mary, a young person of rank, with only a moderate fortune, and Lucy Blakeney, the orphan, depending on the kindness of Mr. Matthews. Another circumstance contributed to the mistake. Miss Blakeney, though her guardian allowed her a very handsome stipend for clothes and pocket money, was yet extremely simple in her attire, her apparel was ever of the best quality, but it was unostentatious, no display of splendor, no glitter or finery disfigured her interesting person; and she scarcely ever purchased a handsome article of dress for public occasions, without presenting something of the same kind, perhaps more elegant or of a finer texture than her own, to her friend Miss Melville, yet she contrived to do this without its being observed, for in all their little shopping parties, Aura was uniformly pursebearer, as Lucy used laughingly to say, to save herself trouble, but in reality to hide her own liberality.

Franklin then easily fell into the common error; and charmed with the person and manners of Miss Blakeney, feeling how proud and happy he should feel to raise so lovely a young woman from dependence to a state of comparative affluence, he determined to scrutinize her conduct, mark her disposition, and should all agree with the captivating external, to offer her his hand, and devote his life to her happiness. Lucy Blakeney, had she been really a destitute orphan, would, when she perceived Franklin's attentions to be serious, and supposed that he imagined her to be an heiress, have insisted on Mr. Matthews' explaining her real situation; but when the reverse was the case, what woman but would have felt highly flattered by the attention of one of the handsomest officers of the corps to which he belonged, a man of honor, and perfect rectitude of conduct, high in the esteem of personages of the first rank, and known to be in possession of a handsome fortune who thus avowedly loved her for herself alone?

Mr. Matthews had a little spice of romance in his composition, and although he did not withdraw the veil from Miss Blakeney's situation, he would have shrunk with horror from the idea of obtaining a splendid alliance for Aura upon the false supposition of her being an heiress.

But there was no immediate call on the integrity of the conscientious guardian on this account. Though numerous were the moths and summer flies who, in expectation of a rich remuneration flitted round Aura Melville, she kept them at such a distance, that they neither disturbed her peace or annoyed her in anyway. They were all treated alike, sometimes listened to with perfect nonchalance, sometimes laughed at, and often mortified with an hauteur which bordered on contempt.

VI

A RENCONTRE, A BALLS LOVE
AT FIRST SIGHT

It was on one of those mornings when the visitants of Brighton sally forth to ransack libraries, torment shopkeepers, and lounge upon the Stiene, when Edward Ainslie taking Lucy under one arm and lady Mary under the other, having taken a walk upon the downs, strolled into one of the public libraries, where raffles, scandal and flirtation were going forward amongst an heterogeneous crowd, assembled there.

At the upper end of the room sat an elderly gentleman in a military undress; apparently in very ill health; beside him stood an elegant fashionable woman, evidently past the meridian of life, but still bearing on her countenance traces of beauty and strong intellectual endowments. Ainslie and his party had been conducted by the master of the shop to seats near these persons.

"I wonder where Mr. Franklin is?" said lady Mary, as she seated herself, "he has neglected us all last evening and this morning, and I shall scold him well when I see him again."

"I have no doubt," said Lucy, "but Mr. Franklin can give a very good account."

"Heavens!" exclaimed the lady who stood by the military invalid. "What is the matter, my dear? Oh! pray make way, let him have air, he is very weak."

Lucy looked round, the veteran had sunk upon the shoulder of his wife, pale and almost lifeless. Having some *eau de Luce* in her hand which she had just before purchased, Lucy stepped forward and presented it to the languid sufferer. The volatile revived him, he opened his eyes, and gazing wildly on Lucy, pushed her hand away exclaiming.

"Take her away, this vision haunts me forever, sleeping or waking, it is still before me."

At that moment lieutenant Franklin broke through the crowd, that filled the room, and giving Ainslie and the ladies a slight bow of recognition, helped the poor invalid to rise, and assisted by the lady, led him to a carriage which waited at the door of the shop, the footman helped him in, and Franklin handing in the lady sprang in after them, and it drove off.

"Who is he?" "What is the matter?" was the general inquiry. Ainslie's party merely heard that it was a brave veteran, who had served many years abroad, and received a wound, from the effects of which he still continued to suffer, and that he sometimes labored under slight fits of insanity. Lucy's eyes filled. She thought of serjeant Blandford. "But what is his disabled limb," said she mentally, "compared to the sufferings of this brave officer? Blandford has but a poor cottage and the pay of an invalid, 'tis true, but he is cheerful and even happy. This poor gentleman appears to be surrounded with affluence, but yet is miserable."

Ainslie sighed as he led them from the library, but made no remark. While lady Mary said,

"Dear! what a pity that a man who has so beautiful an equipage, should be so sick and unhappy. Only think how elegant his liveries were, and how richly the arms were emblazoned on the panels of the carriage." Lady Mary had become skilful in the language of heraldry, under the tuition of her mother, who doated on rank, pedigree, &c., and could have held forth for hours on the crest, supporters, mottoes, and heraldic bearings of most of the noble families in England.

"Who was that young lady who offered your father the *eau de Luce,* and to whom you bowed this morning Jack," asked the mother of Franklin, as he sat tete a tete with her after a melancholy dinner on the evening of the day in which the events just related took place.

"A Miss Blakeney, a very amiable girl under the protection of the Rev. Mr. Matthews, who with his wife, and her sister, the honorable Mrs. Cavendish, and two young ladies to whom he is guardian, are passing, a few weeks in Brighton. They are a charming family. I wish my father's health would permit my bringing you acquainted with them."

"It is impossible," said his mother, sighing, "for besides that the health of your dear father is in a very precarious state, I fear that he has something heavy at his heart; he is much altered, Jack, within the last few months; his rest is disturbed, and indeed it is only by powerful opiates that he obtains any, and by them alone the smallest exhilaration of spirits."

"His wound is no doubt very painful, my dear madam," replied the son, "but we will hope that change of scene, and strict attention to the advice of the medical gentlemen who attend him, will in time restore him."

At that moment the colonel's bell summoned his servant, and the mother of Franklin flew to the apartment of her husband, to strive to alleviate his sufferings by her tenderness and cheer him by her conversation.

"Where was I, Julia," said the colonel, "when that faintness seized me?"

"At the library near the Stiene, my dear. Do you not recollect the interesting girl who presented her smelling-bottle?"

The colonel put his hand to his head, spoke a few words in an under voice, and leaning back on a sofa on which he was seated, closed his eyes, and his wife continuing silent, he dropped into a perturbed slumber.

"We will return to London," said he on awaking "we will set off tomorrow, and then make an excursion to Margate and Ramsgate; from thence to Belle vue, where we will finish the summer."

"Why not go to your sister's for a few weeks? she will be much disappointed if we do not make her a visit this season."

"What, to Hampshire? No, no! I cannot go to Hampshire."

The next morning. Mr. Franklin having breakfasted with and taken leave of his parents, they set off from Brighton, where they had been but three days, in the vain hope that another place would contribute to restore the health and spirits of the colonel.

As the delicacy of every member of Mr. Matthews' family forbade the smallest recurrence to the rencontre in the library with the invalid officer, who, they had learned, was the father of Lieutenant Franklin, when, two days after, he mentioned the departure of his parents from Brighton, no remark was made, but the kind wish offered that his health might soon be restored.

The officers upon duty at Brighton having receives many civilities from numerous families of distinction, temporary residents there, determined, as it drew near the close of the season, to give a splendid ball. Mr. Matthews' family were among the invited guests. Lady Mary was wild with delight; even Lucy felt somewhat exhilarated at the idea of a ball where all the splendor and fashion of the place would assemble, and where it was expected some personages of exalted rank would make their appearance.

Aura Melville was the most stoical of the trio, though it must be confessed her heart did palpitate a little quicker than usual, when Edward Ainslie requested to be her partner the first two dances. Perhaps those quickened pulsations will in some measure account for the perfect indifference with which she had listened to all her admirers.

Balls in anticipation, and indeed in reality, are very pleasant to those engaged in them, but most insufferably dull in detail. It will therefore be sufficient to say that our three orphans enjoyed themselves extremely well.

The attentions of Franklin to Lucy were very pointed. So much so, that Mr. Matthews was resolved, should they continue, and the lieutenant follow them into Hampshire, to call upon him for an explanation of his intentions, and candidly state to him Miss Blakeney's real situation; in order that, should a union take place, such settlements might be made as should secure to her independence for life, whatever events might hereafter happen.

The morning after the ball, lady Mary held forth for a full hour upon the splendid appearance, gallant manners, and evident admiration of a young baronet, who had danced, flirted and flattered, till he had stirred up a strange commotion in her little vain heart. Lucy heard her and smiled. Aura smiled too, but it was with a look of arch meaning, while she replied to the often repeated question of, "Do you not own he is very handsome?"

"Why, yes, as far as tolerable features, good eyes and teeth, with more than tolerable dress goes, I think he is passable; but, my dear lady Mary, he has no noble blood in his veins: his grandfather was *only* Lord Mayor of London, and you know you told me your mother would not rest in her grave if you matched with aught below nobility.

"Now Sir Stephen Haynes' father, and his father before him, were only stationers and booksellers; and who knows, my pretty Mary—*lady* Mary, I beg your pardon—who knows but this very Sir Stephen Haynes may on the female side be a collateral descendant of the renowned Whittington, who made such a fortunate voyage to St. Helena with his *cat?*"

"How do you know it was to St. Helena, Aura?" said Mr. Matthews, looking up, for he had been reading in the parlor where the young folks were talking over the events of the preceding evening.

"Oh! I only surmised, sir, because I read in some geographical work that the island of St. Helena was infested with rats, so that the inhabitants could neither raise or preserve grain of any kind upon it, in which ease, a cat must have been a very valuable animal."

Lady Mary would have left the parlor in a pet, but that she hoped the baronet would call in the course of the morning. He did so, and exercised the art of flattery so successfully, that Mary Lumly totally forgot the expressions of her dying mother, about her degrading herself by a plebeian marriage, and began to think she could be well content to be lady Mary Haynes, though her husband was not a sprig of nobility.

Mr. Matthews had the interest and happiness of each of the orphans under his guardianship much at heart. He thought that Mary Lumly had many good natural qualities; he saw they had been injured by the injudicious conduct of her mother, he had endeavored to rectify some of her romantic notions, and in some measure he had succeeded, but he knew enough of human nature, to be quite aware that when love and romance unite in the mind of a volatile young woman, there is scarcely a possibility of restraining her from taking her own way. Yet he felt it his duty to inquire into the circumstances of the baronet.

In three months lady Mary would be her own mistress, and though her fortune was but trifling, yet, settled on herself, it might secure to her those comforts and conveniences of life to which she had ever been accustomed. He found upon inquiry, that Sir Stephen Haynes, though the only son of a wealthy city knight, had pretty well dissipated his patrimony, and of the many thousand pounds and hundred acres he had inherited from his father, all that remained was Walsteid Hall, a handsome seat in Wiltshire, with gardens, pinery, and farms for pasturage and tillage annexed, but which was deeply mortgaged; so that his whole income at that period would not amount to seven hundred pounds a year.

"Mary Lumly has good sense," said he to himself, "I will speak to her upon this momentous subject. For what will her seven thousand pounds do? It will not clear him of incumbrances, and when it is gone, what is she to do? Mary," said he, addressing her one morning when she was alone with him in the breakfast parlor, "does this young man, who is such a favorite with you, aspire to your hand?"

"He loves me, sir," replied she, "he has a noble estate in Wiltshire, is the only son of a good family, and is willing to make any honorable arrangements previous to our union."

"You have then agreed to accept him?"

Lady Mary looked foolish. "I—I have not refused him, sir."

"Well, Mary, allow me to tell you that he is a bankrupt in both fortune and character. He has lost large sums at the gaming table, has associated with abandoned women and unprincipled men. Can you hope for happiness in a union with such a person?"

"He may, and I have no doubt will reform, sir."

"*May* is barely possible, *will* hardly probable. Men who in early life have associated with profligate women, form their opinion of the sex in general, from that early knowledge. They will not believe any woman capable of resisting temptation, or practising self-denial on principle, because they have found dissolute wives, and easy conquests in young women who are void of religion and virtue. Such men, Mary, may from passion, or from interest, protest that they love you:—But, the passion gratified, the interested motives either complied with or disappointed, ('tis of no consequence which,) the stimulus loses its force, and the ardent lover sinks into the domestic tyrant, or the unfeeling savage."

"I cannot think, sir," said lady Mary, "that Sir Stephen will degenerate into either."

"I would hope, Mary Lumly," he replied, "that you will not take a step of such consequence to your future peace as a matrimonial union, without exercising, not only your own understanding, but consulting me, the guardian under whom you were placed, and whose knowledge of the world will enable him to direct you to avoid those rocks and quicksands on which the voyagers of youth and inexperience are liable to be wrecked. I am very earnest in this cause; I know the delicacy with which you have been brought up; I am well acquainted with the dangerous, I had almost said weak sensibility to which you too frequently yield. It is my duty as your guardian, to take care that a proper settlement be made before you are married."

"I shall not marry directly, sir," said she, "and believe in a short period the law will consider me of an age to dispose of my own person, and take care of my own interest."

"That is very true," said Mr. Matthews, with a sigh, "but let me conjure you, lady Mary, not to be precipitate. Consult your friends. Be advised by those who love you. Ill could you support the deprivations a dissipated, heartless husband may bring upon you: dreadful would be the pangs that would agonize your heart, when that husband should treat with contempt and coldness, the woman he now pretends to idolize."

"I cannot believe either possible, sir."

"May you never find the suggestions realized, my poor child. I will however see Sir Stephen, and speak to him," continued Mr. Matthews.

"I must beg you will not," said the young lady, petulantly. "Sir Stephen's views must be disinterested. What is my paltry fortune to his estates and possessions? he says he does not want a shilling with me."

"Then, Mary, let him prove the truth of his assertion by settling the whole of your fortune on yourself."

"What, sir! when his mind is liberal, shall I prove myself a narrow-minded, selfish wretch, who has no confidence in the man she is about to make her husband? No, sir, when I make him master of my person, I shall also give him possession of my property, and I trust he is of too generous a disposition ever to abuse my confidence." Lady Mary left the room almost in tears, and Mr. Matthews, in order to compose his temper, which had been some what irritated by this unpleasant discussion, walked towards the Stiene.

"What is the matter, lady Mary?" said Miss Blakeney, as she encountered her young associate on the stairs.

"Oh, nothing very particular; only my guardian has been lecturing me about Haynes: as if a young woman nearly twenty-one was not competent to eon duct herself and judge of her own actions."

"Why, as to that," replied Lucy, smiling, as they entered the drawing-room together, "some women are not adequate to the task at forty: but jesting aside, I sincerely hope you will not take any decided step in this business contrary to the advice of Mr. Matthews. You have scarcely known Sir Stephen Haynes a fortnight, and are almost a stranger to his temper, habits and principles."

"You are nearly as much a stranger to lieutenant Franklin, and yet I do not think that you would refuse him if he offered himself."

"You are mistaken, lady Mary; I have no idea of romantic attachments, and laugh when I hear of love at first sight. I should never accept of any man without the approbation of Mr. Matthews and my guardian. Sir Robert Ainslie; and I must have taken leave of my senses, before I should enter into engagements with a young man not quite twenty; for I understand Mr. Franklin is nearly a year younger than myself."

Here the conversation was interrupted by the entrance of the elder ladies and Aura Melville; pleasurable engagements occupied the remainder of the day, and no incident of consequence took place while they continued at Brighton.

About the middle of September, they returned to their delightful residence near Southampton, and for two months, Ainslie, Haynes, and Franklin, appeared not in the family circle. The first attended his father to London; the second was on the turf, dashing away upon the credit of intending soon to marry lady Mary Lumly, whom he represented as a rich heiress; and the third confined to Brighton by his remaining term of duty.

VII

Folly, Rectitude, A Visit to Serjeant Blandford

"Where in the world can Mary Lumly be?" said Mrs. Cavendish, as the evening drew in, and the chill air of October reminded the inmates of Mr. Matthews' mansion, that no one could be walking for pleasure at that hour. Lady Mary had gone out in the morning, expressing her intention of spending the day with Miss Brenton. Now, as it was customary for Mrs. Brenton's servant to attend the young lady home if she stayed to a late hour, the family did not feel much alarmed until ten o'clock approached. Mr. Matthews broke off a game of chess he was playing with Lucy, and looked at his watch; Aura paced the room, and the two elder ladies expressed much uneasiness.

At length a ring at the gate made them start Mr. Matthews in his anxiety preceded the servant to the door, and was well convinced by the precipitate retreat of the person who accompanied lady Mary that it was no menial; nay, he fancied that he saw him kiss her hand, as he opened the door for her admittance.

"You are imprudent, Mary," said the anxious guardian, "to be out so late on this chilly evening, and with such slight covering. Who was the person who parted from you at the door?"

"A gentleman who dined at Mrs. Brenton's."

"And does lady Mary Lumly allow herself to be escorted the distance of nearly a mile in an unfrequented read, at this hour, by a stranger?"

"He was no stranger to Mrs. Brenton, sir."

"Nor to you, Mary, or I am mistaken."—

"I have seen him before," said she, hesitating. "I have met him several times"; and taking a light from the sideboard where several were placed, she left the room.

"Mary will throw herself away," said Mrs. Matthews.

"Then she must abide the consequences," replied Mrs. Cavendish.

"Ah, much I fear," rejoined her sister, "the punishment will exceed the offence. That may be committed in a moment of romantic folly; but the bitter repentance that will succeed, may last through a long and miserable life."

Soon after Christmas, which no circumstances whatever would have prevented Mr. Matthews from celebrating in his own mansion and at his own church, the family removed to London, where a handsome ready furnished house in Southampton street, Bloomsbury square, had been taken for them by Sir Robert Ainslie. Here Sir Stephen Haynes renewed his visits, but generally took care to call when he was sure of meeting other company, and assiduously avoided giving Mr. Matthews an opportunity of speaking to him alone. His manners to lady Mary were polite, but distant, and her guardian began to surmise that he had altered his plans, and had some wealthier prize in view; he was therefore thrown off his guard, and determined to take no further notice of the subject to his fair ward.

The seventeenth of February was lady Mary's birthday, that ardently desired day which freed her from the trammels of restraint, and made her, as she joyously expressed it when Lucy and Aura affectionately kissed her and gave their congratulations, a free and independent agent.

"Then," said Aura, seriously, "I hope you will remain so at least for some years: enjoy this liberty you seem to prize so much; for, be assured, there are shackles much less endurable than the salutary restraints of the excellent Mr. Matthews and his revered wife and sister, and not so easily thrown off."

At one o'clock, the writings necessary being prepared, lady Mary was put in possession of her little fortune. When all was finished, Mrs. Matthews expressed her hope that she would remain in their family at least during the ensuing summer.

She answered, formally, that "she had not yet determined how she should dispose of herself; she should remain with them during the time she stayed in London, and then in all probability make a visit to her friend Miss Brenton."

About three weeks after this event, lieutenant Franklin made a short visit to London, and paid his respects to Lucy and her guardian's family, lamenting that as his father's ill health obliged him to pass the winter in Bath, he could not have the pleasure of making her acquainted with persons she was prepared so highly to esteem. "And for myself, Miss Blakeney," continued he, "I shall not be so happy as to see you above once more, as I have only a fortnight's leave of absence, and must devote the larger part of that time to attentions to my suffering father, and in striving to soothe and cheer the depressed spirits of my mother. But in

June, I hope, my dear sir," turning to Mr. Matthews, "to be permitted to pay my respects to you in Hampshire."

Mr. Matthews expressed the pleasure it would give him to see him there, reflecting at the same time that at the period of the intended visit, he should decide upon the conduct to be observed in developing his intentions towards Lucy.

It was now determined that before Easter, Mr. Matthews and his family should return to their pleasant residence near Southampton. Lucy and Aura were delighted to leave London and return to inhale the sweets of the opening spring and invigorating breezes from the sea. Lady Mary appeared indifferent; but three days before their intended departure, she showed Miss Blakeney a letter which she had received from Miss Brenton, which stated that she was going to pass Easter with an aunt who lived near Windsor, and entreated lady Mary to accompany her.

"I never was at Windsor, Miss Blakeney, and I should like to see that celebrated castle. I have heard my poor mother talk of it."

As lady Mary pronounced the words, *poor mother,* a deep blush suffused her face and neck, and her voice faltered almost to a sob, as she finished the sentence. Lucy Blakeney did not want discernment; she looked earnestly at lady Mary, and catching her hand, said tenderly, yet emphatically,

"But do not go to see it now, dear Mary; go with us into Hampshire, and I promise you when I am of age, which you know will be soon, we will make a most delectable excursion; take dear Guardy and Ma Matthews, majestic Mrs. Cavendish and our lively Aura, and setting out in search of adventures, storm Windsor Castle in the course of our route; and you shall repeat all your lamented mother told you, for you know she was better acquainted with history than we are, especially when it was anything concerning kings and princes, dukes and lords."

Now all this was said in a playful, good-humored manner: But at her heart Lucy feared this excursion with Miss Brenton would lead to no good.

"I cannot retract my promise, dear Lucy," said Mary, in a soft tremulous voice; "Miss Brenton will be in town tonight, and will call for me tomorrow as she proceeds to Windsor."

"Would it not have been as well to have consulted"—Lucy would have proceeded, but lady Mary stopped her with, "I cannot consent to ask leave of the stiff Mr. Matthews, his precise lady, and the dictatorial Mrs. Cavendish."

"Oh fie! lady Mary," replied Lucy, with something of sternness in her voice: "can you forget the parental kindness they have shown you for five years past? You will say, perhaps, the interest of your fortune paid for your board, &c. True, those pecuniary debts were amply discharged. But who can repay the debt of gratitude due to those who cultivate the best feelings of the heart, and direct the understanding to the highest sources of improvement; whose precept and example go hand in hand to lead inexperienced youth into the path of happiness?"

"I never shall forget what I owe them, Miss Blakeney," she replied, "but I cannot consent to solicit permission to do what I like, and go where I please, from persons who, however good in their way, have no right now to control me. I shall myself mention my intention to the family, at the breakfast table tomorrow morning. Miss Brenton will commence her journey about noon, and will call for me; in the mean time I must beg it as a favor, you will not disclose this conversation to anyone."

When she had left the room, Lucy stood for a moment irresolute what course to pursue. "It will do no good," said she mentally, "to distress the family by mentioning this intended excursion, which, however they may disapprove, they cannot prevent; and perhaps I judge too hardly of lady Mary, when I think there is someother point in view than merely visiting Windsor Castle." Thus resolving upon silence, she joined the family at dinner, and found, to her surprise, that lady Mary had complained of a headache, and requested to have some trifling refreshment in her own apartment.

The next morning at breakfast, no lady Mary appeared; and when the footman was desired to send one of the female servants to call her, he replied,

"Lady Mary is not in the house."

"Not in the house!" cried Mr. Matthews, starting from his chair; "poor stray lamb, I fear the shepherd too easily gave up his trust, and thou wilt return no more to the fold."

Mrs. Matthews turned deadly pale, and leaned back in her chair.

"It is no more than I expected," said Mrs. Cavendish, drawing herself up and taking a cup of tea from the trembling hand of Aura.

"Be not too much alarmed," said Lucy Blakeney; "I believe lady Mary was engaged in a pleasurable excursion to Windsor, with Miss Brenton, who arrived in town last evening, and was proceeding thither to visit her aunt. She mentioned it to me yesterday, but said they should

　　　　　　　　SUSANNA ROWSON

not leave town till noon, and that at breakfast she would take leave of the family. Perhaps her friend went earlier than she expected, and Mary Lumly did not like to have the family disturbed; but I have no doubt she has left some letter or message."

"Lady Mary left the house at four o'clock in the morning," said the footman: "she went out through the area, because she was afraid of making a noise to alarm anyone: the chaise did not draw up to the house, but stood at the bottom of the street. Betty, the housemaid, took her bandbox, and I carried her trunk, when, on her jumping in, I saw she was received by a gentleman, and a lady seemed to be in the farther corner. There were four horses to the chaise, and a groom in livery followed it on horseback. 'To Windsor,' said the gentleman, as the door was shut, and they went off like lightning."

"Call Betty this instant," said Mr. Matthews. Betty appeared. "Where is lady Mary Lumly gone?" said he.

"To Windsor, with her friend Miss Brenton," she replied, pertly.

"Did she leave no letter or message, girl?"

"Laws me, yes; there is a letter up stairs for you, I believes."

"Go fetch it, instantly."

"Stop," said he, when the girl gave him a sealed billet; "why did you assist her out of the house in so clandestine a manner? Why not boldly open the front-door, have the carriage drawn up, and call one of my servants to have adjusted her baggage, and if necessary to have proceeded with her?"

"'Cause the poor dear lady cried, and said you and my ladies there wanted to make a slave of her, when she was as free to act for herself as you was, and if you knew of her going you would try to stop her."

"'Tis well: go!" said Mr. Matthews, waving his hand. Betty withdrew with an impertinent toss of her head, and Mr. Matthews opened the letter. It ran thus:

> Sir,
> "I am sensible you will blame the step I am about to take, but I cannot be happy unless as the wife of Sir Stephen Haynes. Before you will receive this, I shall be considerably advanced on the road to Scotland; not that, being my own mistress, anyone has a right to control me, but I dreaded expostulation, and shuddered at the idea of published banns, or a formal wedding by license, with settlements, lawyers,

and parchments. These things have, I believe, little to do with love.—"

"But they have a great deal to do with prudence, I conceive," said the agitated rector, pausing a moment from the perusal of the letter.

"Sir Stephen," he at length proceeded, "has promised to settle half his fortune on me, as a voluntary act of gratitude, after I am his wife; and, in return for this liberality, I have given my little fortune into his hands. He talks of purchasing a peerage; and I begin to have different ideas of nobility since he has convinced me that all by nature are equal, and that distinctions have been always purchased by some means or other; and what matter is it, whether by fighting for the rights of the monarch, or by advancing money to supply his necessities?

"My dear friend Miss Brenton accompanies me to Scotland. I shall, after a short tour, visit her in Hampshire, then, having taken a view of Sir Stephen a place in Wiltshire, and given our orders for repairs, new furnishing, &c., we shall make an excursion of a few months to the continent. On our return we shall pay our respects to you in Hampshire, and solicit a visit from any of the inmates of your mansion who may feel disposed so to honor us. I beg you to accept my thanks for your care of my interest and happiness, although we happened not to think alike upon the latter subject, and make my acknowledgments to Mrs. Matthews and the other ladies of the family for their kind attentions.

I am, sir, with respect and esteem,
MARY LUMLY

Mr. Matthews folded the letter. "The die is cast," said he; "poor Mary Lumly, thou art fallen into bad hands. Settle half his fortune!— according to the course he has pursued, by this time he may not have an acre of land, or a single guinea he can call his own. That Miss Brenton has been of great injury to the unfortunate girl; for nothing can be more prejudicial to a young woman of strong imagination and ill-regulated feelings, than those kind of artificial friendships and tender confidences, where flattery is substituted for real affection, and mutual self-complacency for disinterested attachment; where self-willed folly is dignified with the name of enthusiastic liberality of sentiment, and the excitement of gratified vanity is mistaken for unchangeable, exalted love; such, I am persuaded, was the only friendship that subsisted between Julia Brenton and our thoughtless Mary Lumly; and by her she has been led on to adopt the idea of "all for love, or the world well lost," and to act upon that mischievous, I could almost say dissolute principle."

"I always knew Lady Mary to be vain and thoughtless, and, from the romantic bias given to her early ideas, easily led and highly enthusiastic," said Aura Melville, "but I do believe her mind is pure."

"There is the misery of it!" said Mr. Matthews, sighing; "for when that pure mind shall discover that it has allied itself to sensuality and profligacy, that it has chosen for its associate a being who will divide his time between jockeys and gamesters, and that he is never so happy as when in company with men and women of low breeding and gross conversation, what must it feel?"

No answer was made. The breakfast was removed almost untasted. No steps, however, could be taken to prevent this ill-starred union. Mr. Matthews walked to Sir Robert Ainslie's, and discovered that the whole of Lady Mary's fortune had been the day before withdrawn from his hands, where it had been placed by her guardian on delivering up his trust, by an order under her own signature.

"What, all?—principal, and the few hundreds of interest I had saved for her, that she might have a little store to supply her purse upon coming of age?"

"All," replied Sir Robert "I was not aware of the circumstance till this morning, and was preparing to call on you when you were announced. The order was in favor of Julia Brenton. There was no authority by which we could refuse to pay it."

"Certainly not," said Mr. Matthews, "but she has ruined herself."

The second morning after this very painful occurrence, Mr. Matthews' family set off towards home, where they arrived in safety, and with real pleasure took possession of their old apartments, and began to pursue their usual avocations in that beloved mansion; reading, working, walking, arranging their plants and flowers in the garden and green-house, and occasionally riding round the country, accompanied by their paternal friend the rector.

Mr. Matthews took an early opportunity to call on Mrs. Brenton, but the old lady knew nothing of her daughter's plans, having received but one letter from her since her departure. That indeed was dated from

Windsor, but she appeared totally ignorant of the marriage of Lady Mary, or the active part her daughter had taken in the affair.

Lucy and Aura recommenced their rambles to the cottages of their poor neighbors, nor was the old sergeant forgotten; and be it known, that though Miss Blakeney sometimes thought that June would increase their party, yet was she never heard to complain of the leaden wings of time, or to sigh profoundly, and look interestingly sentimental.

The latter end of June brought Sir Robert Ainslie's family to their seat in Hampshire, and a few days after, Lieutenant Franklin, to visit his friend Edward.

"Lucy, my love," said Mr. Matthews, a few days after the arrival of these young men in their neighborhood, "will you candidly answer me one question, and seriously make me one promise?"

"I will answer any question you may please to make, very honestly, my dear sir," said she, smiling "and as to promises, I am convinced you would require none but what was meant to secure my happiness."

"Now, my good girl, to put you to the test, has Mr. Franklin ever made any professions to you, or sought more than by general attentions to engage your affections?"

"Never, sir: Mr. Franklin never uttered a syllable to me that could be construed into anything more than that politeness and gallantry which gentlemen of his profession think incumbent upon them to pay to our sex." A slight blush tinged her face as she spoke.

"But, my dear Lucy, have you never thought those polite gallantries, as you term them, were sometimes a little particular?"

"The thought"—she replied with a little hesitation,—"but pray do not think me a vain girl;—I have thought his looks and manner said more than his words."

"Good, ingenuous girl," said the rector; "and you would not be displeased if you found yourself the object of his affection? Well, well," he continued, "I will not insist on an answer to this last question. But now to your promise."

"Name it, sir."

"It is that you will enter into no engagements of a matrimonial kind till you have seen your twenty-first birth-day. I have a letter in my possession, written by your grandfather in the last hour of his life. It was designed to be delivered to you when your minority ended; you surely remember how very suddenly that good man was called out of time into eternity."

"Can I ever forget it?" replied Lucy, with emotion. "He had retired to his study, as all imagined, for a few hours' repose, which it was his custom to take of an afternoon, and was found dead in his easy-chair, I think I was told with a written paper before him, and the pen still between his fingers."

"It was so, my child. I was in the house at the time, where I arrived after he had retired; and that paper was an unfinished letter to you. Promise me, therefore, Lucy, that you will enter into no serious engagements till you have read that letter."

"I do promise most solemnly; and also voluntarily add, that every behest in the letter of that dear lamented parent, shall be adhered to by me."

"I know I can depend on you," replied Mr. Matthews, "and am satisfied."

A few days after this conversation, Franklin, having taken his tea at the rectory, proposed a walk, and Aura being engaged in some domestic concerns which Mrs. Matthews had requested her to see performed, Lucy accepted the invitation.

"I will take this young soldier to the cottage of my old friend, serjeant Blandford," said she to Mr. Matthews, "and he shall tell him some of his famous stories, and fight over his battles."

It was a very fine evening, but as the sun descended, a dark cloud received the glorious orb, which, as it shrouded his beams, transfused their radiance into itself, making the edges of its deep purple tint flame with gold and crimson.

"That cloud foretels a shower, I think," said Lucy, as, approaching the old man's dwelling, she turned her eyes for the first time towards the declining sun.

"It will not come on very rapidly," said Franklin.

"We will make a short visit to the old soldier," said she. Then, looking steadfastly at the advancing cloud, she continued, "That cloud is an emblem of misfortune overwhelming for a while the virtuous; which, though for a time it may prevent their general usefulness, and obscure the splendor of their actions, cannot entirely hide their brilliancy, but catches, as it were, a glory from the radiance it partially obscures."

"Or rather," said Franklin, "it is like a veil thrown over the face of a beautiful woman, which shades, but cannot diminish her loveliness."

Before they reached old Blandford's hut, the cloud had spread rapidly, and large drops of rain had fallen, so that Lucy's muslin dress was but a poor defence, and was easily wet through. She had thrown a black lace mantle over her shoulders when she began her walk, but, pulling it off as she rushed into the house, and at the same time divesting her head of a straw cottage bonnet, her redundant hair fell over her face and shoulders.

"Bless me! is it you, Miss Blakeney?" said the old man, rising and supporting himself with his crutch.

"Yes, it is, good Blandford, and finely wet I am; but I use myself so much to all changes of atmosphere, that I do not fear taking cold. I walked very fast when it began to rain, and am incommoded by the heat. So let me sit down, and give me a draught of water."

"Drink sparingly," said Franklin.

At the sound of his voice old Blandford started, and looking first at one and then at the other, asked,

"Who is this, Miss Lucy?"

"My name is Franklin," said the lieutenant, "and I come to visit an old brother soldier." He then presented the veteran his hand, who, gazing earnestly on him, exclaimed, "I could almost have sworn that you were—but I'm an old fool, it is impossible—and this dear lady has often made me think I had seen her face before, though not till this moment could I bring to mind whom she was so like. But just as she is now, only paler and in great distress, I once saw"—he paused—

"Saw whom?" said Lucy.

"It is a melancholy story, miss, and you will not like to hear it, mayhap."

"I have no objection to hear it, if it is not very long, for the rain is almost over, and the moment it ceases, we must set off toward home."

Blandford stretched out his disabled leg, rested his chin on the handle of his crutch, and thus began:—

"You know, Miss Blakeney, I served abroad several years, and got my wound fighting with the—."

"Well, never mind, you have told me all that before; now to your story."

"Why, miss, it was one cold night about the end of October, 1774,—I was but a private then,—when, as I had been to the colonel's quarters for orders, as I went from the door, a poor shivering young creature, her face pale as death, and nothing over her but a thin white gown, and a black something, like that you threw off just now, though the snow was falling fast, and the wind was very bleak—"

Just then Mr. Matthews' carriage drove up to the cottage, and a request was delivered to Miss Blakeney that she would return in it,

　　　　　　　　　　　　　　　SUSANNA ROWSON

as her friends feared she might take cold. The sergeant was therefore obliged to break off his story, when it was scarcely begun, Lucy saying,

"You shall tell it me someother time, my good Blandford, but now goodnight."

Lieutenant Franklin handed her into the coach, bowing as he laughingly said, "A soldier is not afraid of the damp arising from a trifling shower, so I shall walk back to Sir Robert Ainslie's."

This delicate conduct was not lost upon Miss Blakeney, and raised the young man in the estimation of Mr. Matthews.

A short time after this, Mr. Franklin openly made a declaration of his sentiments to Lucy, who referred him to her guardian for the reason why she could not give a decided answer till her twenty-first birth-day was passed. When Franklin heard that Miss Blakeney was in reality a wealthy heiress, instead of the dependent orphan he had depicted in his own mind, and found that he must adopt her name or relinquish her fortune, he felt something like hesitation; he had already laid aside his own family name and assumed that of his grandfather.

"I will be candid, my dear sir," said he; "happiness to me appears unattainable unless in a union with Miss Blakeney, but I must consult my father, and I fear he will never consent to my changing the venerated name I now bear for any other. You know fortune has not been an object with me, for I loved and would have married your ward, though she had nothing but her invaluable self to bestow; but I cannot reconcile it to my own sense of integrity to despoil her of so fair an independence, which entitles her to those appendages and elegances, which my moderate fortune could not afford."

"You are a worthy young man," said Mr. Matthews; "persevere in this course of integrity, and perhaps things may turn out so as to obviate these difficulties. At any rate you will avoid self-reproach; and happiness is so hardly attainable in this world, that it would be a pity, while too eagerly pursuing it, to run the risk of mingling gall with the honey."

When Franklin took leave of Lucy, she held out her hand, and he pressed it to his lips. Her eyes were evidently full, while with a tremulous voice she said,

"Remember, I have entered into no engagements; and whatever the import of my grandfather's letter may be, I am firmly resolved to abide by his directions. You have requested leave to commence a correspondence; you must allow me to decline it. It could be of no service. When the time comes that I shall see this formidable letter, you shall hear either from Mr. Matthews or myself the result: and let that be what it may, I shall ever retain a most grateful sense of your disinterested attachment, and if no nearer tie can ever connect us, I shall ever regard you as a friend and brother."

She then hastily left the room, and shut herself in her own apartment, to give vent to feelings she was unwilling to have witnessed, though she was unable to suppress. Franklin returned to Sir Robert Ainslie's, from whence, at an early hour next morning, he departed with his young friend for London.

VIII

Unpleasant Discovery— Bitter Repentance

Though Sir Stephen Haynes had proposed to the credulous Lady Mary the delightful excursions which she stated in her letter to Mr. Matthews, he never seriously intended any other excursion than the one that made him master of her fortune; and, indeed, could he have obtained possession of that without encumbering himself with her person, he would gladly have done it. When, however, the hymeneal knot was tied, and the romantic, thoughtless girl had paid him the seven thousand pounds, he carelessly asked her if she had reserved any for her own use. Miss Brenton, who was present, not giving her friend time to speak, answered for her, "Certainly, Sir Stephen, Lady Mary has retained a trifle for her pocket expenses, till you have the settlements properly adjusted, and can pay her first quarter."

Sir Stephen looked out of the window and began to whistle. Miss Brenton laid her finger on her lip, looking earnestly at Lady Mary to impose silence upon her; for the truth was, she had persuaded her to retain five hundred pounds, which was the sum Mr. Matthews had mentioned as having laid by for her, during her minority.

"It will be time enough to talk of these things when we have been to Wiltshire," said the new-made bride. "Sir Stephen will then make his own generous arrangements, and I shall not have occasion for much money till I get to London, when I must have an entire new wardrobe, have the few jewels my mother left me more fashionably set—You will have a new carriage, I presume, Sir Stephen," addressing her husband, "and new liveries?"

"I don't know that I shall have either, madam," said he. It was the first time he had ever addressed her by the formal title of madam. She looked at him, and her color varied, but thinking he might suppose that she wished to hurry to London, she said,

"I did not mean that we should go directly there; if we are only there time enough to have everything ready for the birth-day, when I shall expect to be presented by some of my mother's relations."

"Then you will be disappointed," he replied, sharply, "for I do not think I shall go to London at all. It is a devilish expensive place, and you cannot suppose that your fortune entitles you to form such expectations however your ladyship's rank may be."

"I never deceived you in regard to my fortune, Sir Stephen," she answered, her lip beginning to quiver, and a choking sensation to arise in her throat.

"But I suppose you knew that your accommodating friend there had done it; she represented your fortune more than quadruple the paltry sum you have given me."—

"I have given you all, Sir Stephen," said she, "and had it been a thousand times as much, would have given it as freely." She hid her face with her handkerchief, and burst into an hysterical sob.

"Oh, pray don't let us have a crying match so early in the honeymoon," said he. "I hate whimpering; it spoils a pretty face and makes an ugly one detestable." He snatched up his hat, and sauntered out.

It may be easily imagined what a young woman of such uncontrollable feelings as Lady Mary must have endured, at this discovery of the selfish disposition of a man to whom she had intrusted her all of fortune, her all of earthly felicity; she threw herself into the arms of Miss Brenton, and exclaimed,

"Theresa, why have you done this? I thought him disinterested; I thought he loved me for myself; why, why did you lead him to think"— "My dear Mary," said Miss Brenton, soothingly, "how can you blame me? I did not know the extent of your fortune. You were reputed an heiress; your guardian never contradicted the report; and knowing how immensely rich Sir Stephen was left by his father, I rejoiced in the prospect of seeing my dear friend, so amiable, so lovely, united to a man able to add to her exalted rank the gifts of fortune. And when I knew your sensitive heart was engaged by him, I thought, in promoting your union, I was promoting your happiness."

"Forgive my petulance, Theresa," said Lady Mary, drying her eyes, "but what must I do?—how must I conduct myself?"

Let it be remembered that Lady Mary was but a wife of three days; for on their return from Scotland they had stopped at Alnwick in Northumberland, where so much of antiquity and ancient splendor were to be seen, connected with historic tales of chivalry and renown, that Mary Lumly, as she passed through it on her imprudent expedition, had expressed a wish to stop on her return, and view the castle, the gates of the town, and other objects, to which her enthusiastic spirit of romance had given the highest interest.

Accordingly, on the second night of their retrograde journey, they stopped at an old-fashioned but well-attended, comfortable inn, in the ancient town of Alnwick, not very far from the beautiful seat so long descended from father to son in the noble family of Percy, of Northumberland. On the second morning after her arrival there, the scene took place, which led to the question of "What must I do?—how must I conduct myself?"

"Struggle to suppress your feelings," said Miss Brenton; "when Sir Stephen returns, receive him with composure, and on no account let him know of the small sum you have retained, for, from all I see and hear, I suspect it will be sometime before you gain anything from him."

Theresa Brenton was an artful, selfish young woman; her mother was a widow with a small jointure, and Theresa, with a very trifling fortune of her own, looked round for ways and means to lead a life of ease and affluence, without infringing on a small patrimony inherited from her father, except to supply her with necessary articles of clothing and pocket-money. She had early begun to try her talent of flattery upon Lucy Blakeney; but Lucy had too much sense to be led or hoodwinked by soft speeches, and a yielding versatility of manners. She was always polite, and treated Miss Brenton with that suavity of demeanor which was her general characteristic; but she could not love her as an associate, nor confide in her as a friend.

Lady Mary Lumly had been accustomed to the voice of adulation from her earliest remembrance; she had observed how subservient her governess always was to the will of her mother; she never contradicted her, and if at anytime she was unreasonably petulant, from ennui, or irritable nerves, she was always silent, or soothed her into good-humor again. Lady Mary thought this a proof of the strongest affection; she loved her governess, who was equally indulgent to her foibles, and glossed them over with the name of amiable weaknesses.

It may be here observed, that a conduct which was kind and consoling, to a woman formerly followed and courted by an admiring world, moving in the most splendid circles, indulged in every wish of her heart, but who was now weak in health, depressed in fortune, and neglected by that world; it was the height of cruelty to practise toward a young creature just entering into life.

When, after the death of her mother, Lady Mary was removed to the regular, well-conducted family of Mr. Matthews, where a kind of sedate cheerfulness went hand in hand with rational amusement and mental improvement, the change was so great that she was glad to meet a more congenial associate in Theresa Brenton. The consequence was, that they became, in the language of romantic misses, "*sworn friends.*" Lady Mary would complain of the formality of Mrs. Cavendish, the strictness of Mr. Matthews, and the undeviating preciseness of his wife. Miss Brenton would reply, "I feel for you, my dear Mary; it must be very painful to your sensitive mind: but be patient, it cannot last forever, and the time will arrive, when, being your own mistress, you can indulge those amiable sensibilities which throw a fascinating charm around you, and, whilst constituting your own happiness, render you the delight of all who know you."

In the mean time Theresa Brenton would, when Mary Lumly received her quarterly allowance, accompany her, from *pure good-nature*, on her shopping expeditions, and when her friend purchased any elegant or expensive article, would lament that she had not the power to indulge herself in anything beyond usefulness; when often the thoughtless, yet generous-minded Mary would suffer considerable depredations on her purse, rather than dear Theresa should feel the want of an article that would set off her pretty person so well, but which her confined finances would not allow her to purchase.

Miss Brenton was herself deceived in regard to Sir Stephen's fortune, when, following Lady Mary from Brighton, he contrived to get an introduction to the family, where he found he could make a staunch auxiliary by a profusion of protestations and a few showy presents. His equipage and dress were so elegant, his disregard of expense so evident, that both Mrs. and Miss Brenton conceived his revenues to be immense; and Theresa thought, by assisting her *friend* in eluding her guardian's watchfulness and forming a matrimonial union with Sir Stephen, she should secure to herself an invitation to pass one winter at least in London, during which period she might secure an establishment for herself, and, another season, dash forth, at parties, balls, and routs, at the opera, theatre, or masquerade, as the rival or superior of her *angelic friend* Lady Mary Haynes. She therefore pretended not to know the extent of Lady Mary's fortune, but led the scheming, selfish baronet to conclude that it was above twenty thousand pounds.

Mary Lumly herself would have spurned such an imposition, but she never made that mental exertion which is necessary when persons mean to judge and decide for themselves. She had been blindly led by the flattery and opinion of Theresa Brenton, and was taught to believe that in asking for or submitting to the advice of Mr. Matthews, she was making herself a slave to the will of one who, being old and fastidious, was incapable of deciding upon what would constitute be happiness of a young and beautiful woman.

But Theresa Brenton, in abetting the elopement, had overreached herself. She had no idea, when she received, by Lady Mary's order, the whole of her little fortune from Sir Robert Ainslie, that the innocent, confiding girl meant to give it unconditionally to her husband, before he had made the promised settlements, which even at that time she had no doubt he had the power to make. But when she found it impossible to persuade her from so doing, she strongly urged her to retain the five hundred pounds in her own hands.

When dinner was announced, and the ladies met Sir Stephen, Lady Mary strove to smile; Miss Brenton was remarkably cheerful, and when the cloth was removed, he made a proposal to visit Alnwick castle that afternoon. The smiles naturally returned to the face of his bride, and the carriage being ordered, they proceeded to the stately mansion of the Percys.

Sir Stephen knew when he made the proposal, that some of the family being at that time in Northumberland, it was not likely that they would be admitted to view the castle; and when he received for answer, on applying for admittance at the porter's lodge, that there was company there at present, turning to Lady Mary, he said,

"Well, it can't be helped, but we will take a drive round to view a little romantic spot which I am sure you will be pleased with. When I went out this morning, I met a friend I had not seen for many years, who now lives within a short distance of Alnwick; I walked with him to his house, where he resides with his mother, and from thence, on one of his horses, accompanied him on a ride in this delightful country, where there is so much to gratify both the taste and the judgment."

As they rode along, Sir Stephen was uncommonly attentive and entertaining. At an opening from a wood, he pointed out a cottage, built in the antique style, with a garden gay with early spring flowers, and surrounded by a small patch of ground, in which was a variety of beautiful flowering shrubs, though they now only showed their under green leaves. The ladies both exclaimed,

"Well, what a lovely place! it is just a situation to realize the idea of love in a cottage."

Sir Stephen bade the postilion drive up to the gate.

"Come," said he, "we will alight and get some tea here. There will be a fine moon this evening, and we shall have a pleasant drive afterwards." But Miss Brenton observed, "that she thought the road they had come was very lonely; they had seen but few passengers, and those not very prepossessing in their looks."

"Besides," said Lady Mary, "this is certainly not a house of entertainment."

"We shall try that," said he, jumping out; and, insisting on the ladies alighting, he led the way up to an old-fashioned porch, over which climbed the woodbine and sweetbrier, just bursting into vegetation. An elderly woman opened the door and ushered them into a not inelegant, but small parlor.

"Where is Mr. Craftly?" asked Sir Stephen.

"I expect him in every moment, your honor!" said the woman, whom we will call Janet, "and he told me, should your honor arrive before him, to show the ladies their rooms, and obey their orders in everything."

The ladies were struck almost dumb with astonishment. "Our rooms!—why, are we to remain here all night?" faintly articulated Lady Mary.

"Your lady, Sir Stephen, has no night-clothes here," said Miss Brenton, with rather more firmness of voice, "and how can we be accommodated in this little place?"

"Pho! Theresa," he replied, half-jocularly, "don't raise obstacles where none really exist: I have ordered the trunks to be brought. I did not like our situation at the inn, and my friend having offered me the use of this cottage for a short period, I concluded it would just suit Lady Mary's taste; and you know you both declared just now it was exactly the situation to realize the idea of *love in a cottage*."

"True," said Lady Mary, with a slight degree of acrimony, "but I do not know how I shall like the cottage without the love."

At this moment Craftly entered, and Sir Stephen, taking his arm, walked into the little shrubbery.

"What can this mean, Theresa?" inquired the pale and agitated bride. Miss Brenton shrugged her shoulders, but remained silent; and they concluded to go and inspect the apartments.

The cottage consisted of two parlors, a kitchen, and four bed-chambers, neatly but not elegantly furnished.

"I won't stay here," said Lady Mary.

"But how shall we get away?" rejoined her companion, "for I believe the carriage is gone in which we came. But be patient, dear Mary; this may only be a frolic of Sir Stephen's to try your temper. Take no notice, ask no questions, endeavour to be cheerful, and all may be well yet. He knew your mother's attachment to rank and splendor, he may fear that you inherit her family pride."

"I wish to heaven I had!" she ardently replied, "I should never have fallen into this humiliating situation."

"Well, what is done cannot be undone," said Theresa, with a nonchalance surprising to her friend.

At tea, though Lady Mary was calm, she could not be cheerful. Miss Brenton was rather silent and observant. Craftly stayed the evening, and after supper challenged Sir Stephen to a game at piquet. The ladies retired to their chambers, where they found their trunks, but on looking round, Lady Mary missed her dressing-case, in which were her jewels and all her money, except about twenty-five guineas which were in Theresa's purse.

She had inquired into the establishment of the cottage, and found it consisted only of the elderly person she had first seen, who acted as cook and housekeeper and a rude country girl, who was to attend the ladie and take care of the chambers; a half-grown boy, to clean knives and attend at meal-times, and a poor old crone who occasionally came to superintend the garden and grounds. The girl, accustomed to early hours, was gone to bed; the woman thought her work was finished when the supper-table was cleared, and the boy expressed his discontent when he found he must sit up to wait on the gentlemen.

When, therefore, Lady Mary, on retiring to her room, found no one to assist her in undressing, or to go to Sir Stephen to inquire for her dressing-case, Miss Brenton, who felt more alarmed than she was willing to own, snatched up the candle,—for there was but one in the apartment,—and, without apology, hastened back to the parlor.

"Sir Stephen," said she, throwing open the door, "your lady's dressing-case is not come."

"Well," he replied, "what of that? I suppose she can do without it for one night. Lend her some of your things, Theresa, for I believe *they* are come."

"They may be, but I was so disturbed upon missing this valuable case, (for it belonged to your lady's mother, and she prizes it very highly,) that I did not look for, or even think of my own things."

"Well, well, I dare say it is safe enough; I will see about it tomorrow; so, good Theresa, do go now, and leave us to play our game in peace."

"What a fool I have been! and how I have misled poor Lady Mary!" said Miss Brenton, mentally, as she ascended the stairs. But, endeavoring to suppress her feelings, and look cheerful as she entered the room where her friend was undressing, she said,

"The box will be here tomorrow! you must condescend, dear Mary, to use my dressing apparatus tonight, and in the morning, I hope we shall prevail on Sir Stephen to give up the wild scheme of staying anytime in this cottage, and commence a journey, if not to London, at least into Hampshire, where I am sure my mother will be happy to receive you till Sir Stephen can look round and settle in a proper habitation."

After a few remarks, not very pleasant to either party, the ladies separated; but though they retired to bed, sleep visited neither of them till nearly daylight. When it did overtake them, it was so profound that they did not awake till after nine in the morning.

Lady Mary, on looking round, soon perceived that Sir Stephen had not been in bed all night. A vague sensation of desolateness struck upon her heart: she started up, and searched for a bell, but no bell was to be found. She opened the chamber door and called aloud for Theresa, and in a few moments, wrapped only in a dressing-gown, her friend entered the room.

"Sir Stephen has not been in his apartment all night, Theresa; what can be the meaning of this?" she exclaimed, wildly. Before Miss Brenton could reply, Janet, who had been listening, hearing the ladies speak, came up to say that breakfast had been ready above an hour.

"Where is your master, good woman?" asked Miss Brenton, as calmly as she could.

"My master! Mr. Craftly, does your ladyship mean? He walked out with his honor Sir Stephen, before five o'clock, and said he should not return to breakfast; but Dora, when she was cleaning the parlor where their honors played cards last night, sawed this bit of paper; but what it's about we can't tell, for neither she nor I can read joining hand."

Before Janet had finished her harangue, Theresa had snatched the note from her hand, eagerly broke the seed, and read as follows:—

To Miss Theresa Brenton:
  "You cannot be surprised, Theresa, after the explanation which took place between Lady Mary and myself yesterday,

that I should declare my utter inability to make those settlements which I talked of before our excursion to the north. I must beg you to make my acknowledgments to the dear generous girl for all marks of favor and kindness bestowed by her on her unworthy, humble servant; but my finances are in such a state, that it is totally impossible for me to take a journey to Wilts, as proposed, or to solicit her company to France, whither I must repair as speedily as possible, to rusticate, whilst my affairs in England are put in train to restore me to some comparative degree of affluence. My friend, Richard Craftly, Esq., has offered the cottage to you and your lovely friend as long as you may please to occupy it. He is, Miss Brenton, a man of good abilities, amiable disposition, and possessed of a small but genteel and unencumbered estate, which, upon the death of his mother, will be augmented. He will call on you this afternoon. *I recommend him to your notice*. My best wishes attend you and your fair associate, Lady Mary.

> I am, dear Theresa,
> Your obliged friend, &c. &c.,
> STEPHEN HAYNES

"Give it to me!—give me that letter, Theresa!" exclaimed Lady Mary, snatching it from Miss Brenton. Her frenzied eye glanced rapidly over its contents, and muttering,

"*Friend! associate!*—yes, it flashes on my mind, I have no certificate; he gives me no name. I am undone! undone!—Oh! my guardian! my dear, kind Lucy!"

The letter fell from her hand; she clasped her fingers tightly across her forehead, and before the terrified and humane Janet could step forward to catch her, she fell lifeless on the floor.

IX

The Letter—the Birth-day

October had almost expired, and Lucy Blakeney began to count the hours when she should be relieved from the state of suspense in which she was placed, and which, notwithstanding her well-regulated mind and subdued feelings, was very painful. She had occasionally heard through the Ainalie family of Franklin's health, and that his father still remained in a weak and sometimes deranged state. Her mind was harassed; she even no longer took pleasure in visiting Blandford's cottage.

"I cannot account for it, Aura," said she one day to Miss Melville, "but, though my curiosity was awakened by the manner in which the old sergeant commenced his story, yet I cannot summon resolution to ask him to tell it me; a certain terror spreads through my frame, and I wish to hear no more of it till I can hear it in company with Mr. Franklin."

"Alas, and a-well-a-day," replied Aura, laughing, "what a sad thing this tender something is, which we hardly dare own, and know not how to describe."

"Well, I will not deserve to be laughed at, Aura; for I will act upon principle, and am resolved to partake of and enjoy all the comforts and innocent pleasures of life that may fall in my path, though one little thorn should pierce my foot in my pilgrimage."

"Your foot or your heart, Lucy?"

"Why, my good Aura, I shall strive to keep it as far from my heart as I can."

"Do you remember, Lucy, what day next Thursday is?" asked Mr. Matthews one morning, as he sat at breakfast with his family.

"It is my birth-day, sir, is it not?"

"Even so, my good little girl"; for with Mr. Matthews everything that was held very dear by him, was denominated *little*.

"Well," continued he, "and what shall we do to celebrate the day? I have no doubt that all the beaus and misses in the environs of Southampton, have long been anticipating splendid doings on the day when Miss Blakeney obtains her majority."

"I mean to have very splendid goings, sir."

"Indeed!"

"YES"—

"I wonder then, Miss Blakeney, you did not give my brother and sister intimation of your intent," said Mrs. Cavendish, "that proper preparations might have been made, without the hurry which must now ensue."

"Oh, my dear madam," said Aura, "Lucy and I have been busy these two months past in preparing for this interesting occasion, and, indeed, our invitations are already sent out, and everyone, I do assure you, accepted."

"Very extraordinary conduct, I think," said the consequential old lady.

"I wish you had given a little more time," said Mrs. Matthews, mildly, "but, however, we will see what can be done. But what is it to be? a ball and supper? or a breakfast in fashionable style?"

"Oh, neither, madam, though I hope to make some dance and some sing, who are not much in the habit of doing such things."

Mrs. Cavendish had taken a large pinch of snuff, and having wiped the *poudre tabac* from her upper lip with one of her finest colored silk handkerchiefs, which, together with her elegant snuff box, she deposited in a filagree work-basket which always stood beside her, and opened her delicate white cambric one, and laid it on her lap, was beginning to speak, when Mr. Matthews said, "These girls are only playing tricks with us, sister. Lucy no more intends to have a party, than I intend to take a voyage to the moon."

"Don't you be too sure, my dear sir," said Lucy, laying her hand playfully on his arm. "I have really invited a party of forty to dine here on Thursday next; and all I have to ask is that you will lend me the hall, and that Mrs. Matthews will have the goodness to order John to lay the cloth in a simple manner for my guests, and permit the cook and housekeeper for all day on Wednesday to obey my injunctions."

"Well, children," said Mrs. Matthews, "I believe you must have your way this once. It shall be, Lucy, as you wish."

"But come, Lucy," said Mr. Matthews, "let us somewhat into the secret; I suspect you will want a llitte cash to carry your fine plans into effect."

"Not a doit, dear sir, till Thursday morning, when I shall want one hundred pounds in guineas, half-guineas, crowns and half-crowns."

"Extravagant baggage," he replied, his fine, venerable countenance glowing with pleasure. "Now tell us the arrangements of the day."

"Oh, they are very simple. You know, my ever-venerated Mr. Matthews, on that day I expect to read a letter, the contents of which will most probably determine the hue of my future fate." She spoke with solemnity, and a slight convulsive tremor passed over her intelligent features.

"If you please, let that letter remain uninvestigated till I retire for the night. I would enjoy the innocent festivities I have projected for the day,—and now," she continued with more hilarity of manner, "I will tell you my plan. About twelve o'clock I expect my guests to begin to assemble; they will consist of a few of the oldest and most respected poor of your parish, with children and grandchildren. Aura and myself will receive them in the large sitting-parlor, when yourself, with whom I shall deposit my hundred pounds, shall portion it out amongst them according to your judgment; for you must be the most proper person to decide upon their necessities and merits. You have ever been so liberal in your allowance to me, that having laid by a little hoard, Aura and myself have provided garments for the oldest and most infirm, the youngest and most desolate, and suitable presents for the rest."

"Oh ho!" said Mr. Matthews; "so now the secret is out of the cause of the many jaunts to Southampton lately, and the long conferences held in the dressing-room, of a morning early, to which none but a few industrious young women were admitted."

"Even so, sir; for while we were gratifying our own whims, it was but just that they should not be selfish ones; so, when Aura and I had cut the garments, we employed those young persons to make them, so that they might be benefited by forwarding our scheme, without feeling the weight of obligation, which I should think was a feeling most repugnant to the young and active. They have none of them been let into the secret of the use for which these garments are designed, but some of them, if not all, will partake of our festivities."

Mrs. Cavendish had, during this explanation, sat with her eyes fixed on Miss Blakeney's face; she had folded and unfolded her cambric handkerchief several times; her eyes twinkled, she hemmed, applied the before mentioned silk handkerchief to her nose, and at length, reaching her hand across the table, she said, in no very firm voice, "You are certainly a most extraordinary young lady, and I begin to think I have never rightly understood you. Pardon me, child, I fear I have this morning been both illiberal and rude."

"So well acquainted as I am with Mrs. Cavendish's good understanding, and highly cultivated mind," said Lucy, gracefully taking the extended hand, "it would be next to impossible that I could suspect her of ever being intentionally either illiberal or rude."

"Well, well," replied the old lady, with one of her most knowing nods, "I trust I shall know you better in future."

On the Wednesday following, several good sirloins of beef were roasted, hams boiled, pies baked, and or the Thursday morning plumpuddings boiled for the expected regale. It was scarcely twelve o'clock when the company began to assemble; the young brimful of joy, and the old anticipating they hardly knew what; but all were cheerful and blithe with the most delightful sensations. Amongst the first arrived old Alice Lensdale and her good man, brought by one of their neighbors, whom Lucy had engaged for the purpose, in a chaise; nor were Thomas, who had now recovered the use of his limbs, with his good dame and children, forgotten. The family who had excited so warmly Lady Mary Lumly's romantic enthusiasm, were the blithest among the blithe in the happy group, that not only filled the rector's eating-parlor, but partially filled the benches in the great hall; for Lucy's forty, when children, grandchildren, and in some cases great-grandchildren were collected, amounted to about sixty. Dishes of common cake were handed round, with cheese and ale for the men, and wine-sangaree for the women. Mr. Matthews then, with a discriminating hand, portioned out the bounty of the heiress, according to the necessities of all; and many were that day provided with the means of passing through the ensuing winter with comfort, who else must have been pinched, both for fuel and sustenance.

At half-past two the tables were plentifully spread, at which, amongst the elder guests, Mr. and Mrs. Matthews presided, and at that with the younger, sat Lucy and Aura, while Mrs. Cavendish walked round, looked at their happy faces, and took her pinch of snuff with more exhilarated feelings than she had experienced for years before.

After dinner, Lucy and Aura invited the matrons to their own apartments, which adjoined each other, where each received a present of clothing adapted to her age, circumstances, and family. The young ones sported cheerfully in the grounds, the old men talked in groups round the hall chimney, where blazed an old-fashioned, large and cheerful fire. At six, a regale of coffee, tea, and simple cakes, with bread and butter, were set forth; and before eight, all had retired to seek their homes, under the light of a brilliant full moon.

And how did Lucy feel when all were departed? She felt as a Christian ought to feel; she had cheered and enlightened the hearts of many; she had herself enjoyed the purest felicity during the whole day;

and she mentally exclaimed, as, taking the letter from her guardian, she sought her own apartment,

"I have now a bitter cup to drain, let me not repine. I have much, very much, to be grateful for, and what right have I to expect to walk over beds of roses without feeling the briers which surround the stalks on which those beautiful and fragrant flowers blossom?"

She entered her chamber, bidding Aura goodnight at the door, which closing, she sat down, the letter in her hand, which, though unsealed, she had not the courage to open; at length, rallying her spirits, she unfolded the paper and read,

To Miss Lucy T. Blakeney
To be delivered on the day she attains the age of twenty-one.
"From the hour when I closed the eyes of your beloved, ill-fated mother, you, my dear Lucy, have been the delight and solace of your grandmother and myself. And your amiable disposition has led us to hope, that you may in future be the happy inheritress of the estate and property on which we have lived above thirty-five years: happy, my child, in bestowing comfort on others, and doubly happy in the enjoyment of reflected joy from grateful hearts.

"You are in possession of independence from the bequest of Captain Blakeney, but you will find by my will, that it is my wish that not a farthing of that bequest, either principal or interest, should be expended on you during your minority; the income arising from your hereditary estate, &c., being amply sufficient to clothe, board, and educate you, in the style of a gentlewoman. You are by law entitled to the name and arms of Blakeney, but there was a clause annexed to your godfather's will which gave your dear grandmother and myself some uneasiness. It is that which insists that your future husband should change his own name to that of Blakeney, or the whole of the original bequest will be forfeited, and the accumulated interest only be yours.

"My lamented wife, in her last hours, Lucy, said to me, 'I wish, love, you may live to see our lovely child of an age when you may advise her never to shackle her sensibility by feeling as if she were obliged to reject the man whom she may love, and who might make her very happy, because

SUSANNA ROWSON

himself or his friends should object to a change of name. I myself have such a predilection for family names, that had it not been for particular circumstances, and that the name of a female must at sometime or other in all probability be changed, I should never have consented to our Lucy assuming the name of Blakeney. Should you be called hence before she is of a proper age to understand and be intrusted with every necessary communication on the subject of her birth, and other interesting circumstances, I must entreat you will be very explicit with her guardians, and also leave a letter addressed to herself."

"Soon after this conversation, the companion and friend of my life, the heightener of all my joys, the consoler of all my sorrows, the only woman I ever loved, left this transitory sphere for a more blissful region. From that moment the world, my Lucy, has appeared a blank. Not even your endearing cheerfulness, your affectionate sympathy, could call me back to any enjoyment in life. I have endeavored several times to nerve my feelings to the performance of this task, and have blamed myself for thus procrastinating it. But from several symptoms of failure in my mental and bodily vigor, I feel it will not be long before I follow my regretted partner into the world of spirits.

"I expect to see Mr. Matthews in the course of a few weeks; I shall then make him the confidant of many sorrows, which have sunk deep into my heart, and drank its vital energies, earlier than, perhaps, time might have impaired them. I entreat, my Lucy, my last earthly treasure, that in no momentous concern of your life you will act without consulting him, and when you have consulted, abide entirely by his decision.

"As it regards a matrimonial connection, let not the clause of your godfather's will have any influence. Your own patrimony will yield four hundred pounds a year; half this must be settled on yourself. The accumulation of the interest on my friend Blakeney's bequest will be very considerable in eleven years. This is your own, to be settled or disposed of as yourself may direct. I have, by insisting on half your patrimony being settled on yourself previous to the day of marriage, secured to you the comforts and conveniences of life, as long as life may be continued; for the rest, I leave you in the charge of a good and heavenly Protector, who will never leave those to perish, who rely on His Providence.

"There is one thing, my ever dear child, I am very anxious about, and on which my charge to you will be very solemn. It is, that you will never marry any of the name of N——."

Here the stroke of death arrested the hand which held the pen, and the good old gentleman was found, as already mentioned, dead in his easy-chair.—

"What can I think!—how must I act?" said Lucy, as, with stunned faculties, she still gazed on the open letter on the table before her. "I will determine on nothing till I know the opinion of my guardian on the subject; in the mean time I will implore the guidance and protection of Him who knoweth best what is good for his children, and leave the event to time." So concluding, she folded the letter, performed her nightly devotions, and retired to her bed.

Lieutenant Franklin was now in London; his father, whose health was still very feeble, had, with his family, taken up his residence in his house in Portland Place. He had counted the days with anxiety, till the arrival of Lucy's birth-day; after that, time seemed to have added lead to his pinions, and every hour and day was as an hundred. At length he received the following letter from Mr. Matthews:—

To Lieutenant John Franklin

"I have sat down, my dear sir, to fulfil a most unpleasant task, in communicating to you, by the desire of our lovely and esteemed friend, Miss Blakeney, a copy of her grandfather's letter, which I enclose, thinking it best to keep the original in my possession.

"You will perceive that the old gentleman was by no means averse to her marrying to please herself, though it might be to the diminution of her fortune. That there were some unhappy circumstances attending the birth of Miss Blakeney, I have every reason to conclude; though what those circumstances were, I never could ascertain. For, though my respected old friend frequently promised to impart them to me, the communication was deferred from time to time, till with him, poor man, time was no more.

"You will also perceive that there is some particular family into which he had strong objections to her marrying; but the unfinished capital, which I am at a loss to decide whether meant for an N, an M, or an A, leads to no direct conclusion. I know he had a peculiar dislike to a family of the name of Lewis, the descendants of which in one branch are Mertons, in another North-allertons. There was a person also of the name of Allister, who gave him much trouble by a lawsuit. But I can hardly think my old friend was so little of a Christian as to let his prejudice descend from generation to generation. However, be that as it may, there is nothing in the unfinished capital, that looks like F. Miss Blakeney is well, and has kept her birth-day in a most novel and splendid manner. I wish you could have seen her presiding amongst her guests; but I presume it will not be long before we see you at the rectory, when you will hear from every tongue— yes, even from sister Cavendish, her eulogium.

I am, dear sir,
Yours, with esteem,
Alfred Matthews

The evening after Mr. Matthews had despatched this letter, he entered the sitting-parlor, where his family were assembled, some at work, some reading, and Aura Melville strumming, as she called it, on the guitar. He took a morocco case from his waistcoat-pocket, and seated himself by a work-table where Lucy was elaborately plying the needle's art, without having any definite end for which the work was designed when completed. He opened the case; a miniature of a lady, set in wrought gold, and suspended by a superb chain, was taken from it, and, throwing the chain over Lucy's neck, he said,

"This, my little girl, should have been a birth-day present, but you were so happy on that day, I thought you should not have too much satisfaction at once: it is good and prudent to portion out pleasure by degrees. If we are too lavish of it, the sense of enjoyment becomes torpid."

Lucy took the picture; it was that of a lovely female, not more than sixteen years old: on the reverse was a braided lock of brown hair, surmounted by the initials C. T., in fine seed-pearl.

"Who is this lovely creature?" said Lucy.

"Come to the glass, my child, and tell me who it is like," said Mr. Matthews, leading her to the glass, and raising a candle near her face. Lucy looked, and hesitated.

"Only," at length she said, "only that it is much handsomer, and the eyes are blue, I should think"—

"That it was like yourself," said Mr. Matthews, leading her to the sofa, where Aura, having laid aside her instrument, was ready to receive her.

"It is the portrait of your mother, Lucy. It was taken, your grandfather informed me, about three years previous to your birth, and was constantly worn by your grandmother, till some deeply afflicting occurrences, to which I am a stranger, induced her to lay it aside."

Lucy pressed the fair semblance of youth and innocence to her lips and to her heart; tears rushed from her eyes, and, depositing the portrait in her bosom, she rested her head on the shoulder of Aura, and perfect silence for several minutes pervaded the apartment.

"So here is our friend Franklin!" said the good rector, a few mornings after, presenting the young lieutenant to the busy group drawn round the fire-side in the breakfast-parlor.

Franklin bowed, and, with a face half-doubting, half-delighted, took a chair beside Lucy. She smiled, blushed, broke off her thread, unthreaded her needle, threaded it again, and worked most assiduously, without one single idea of why or wherefore. She asked, When he left London? What was the state of his father's health? When he last saw Edward Ainslie? till, without being perceived by them, separately and silently, every person but themselves had left the room.

Of all scenes to be repeated in narrative, love-scenes are the most sickening, silly, and uninstructive. Suffice it to say, that in an hour after they found themselves alone, Lucy had resolved to relinquish the principal of Blakeney's legacy. Franklin, with entire satisfaction, accorded to the terms of settling half her paternal inheritance on herself, and receiving the accumulated interest of eleven years on twenty thousand pounds, as a fortune to be disposed of according as his judgment should direct.

Friendship, love, and harmony now took up their residence in the rectory; the unostentatious though silently progressing preparations making for the wedding of Miss Blakeney, furnished occupation for every female of the family. Even Mrs. Cavendish relaxed her stern, yet really handsome features into smiles, as she gave her opinion upon some new purchase, or told the young persons whom Lucy chose to employ on this occasion, how such and such a dress was made and trimmed when she was some few years younger.

It was one of Miss Blakeney's eccentricities, that nothing that could be performed by the industrious young women in the immediate vicinity of the rectory, should be sent for from London; and one morning, when Mrs. Matthews and Mrs. Cavendish argued that her outward garments might be more tasteful and fashionable if made in the metropolis, she replied,

"But I am so vain as to think I should not look any handsomer in them, and I am sure I should not feel so happy. I know these good young women; some of them have aged parents to support, some young brothers and sisters to educate and put in a way to get their own bread. I am very sensible that, with the assistance of Miss Melville and our female domestics, more than two-thirds of the work that is to be done, might be performed without any additional expense. But it has been a principle with me, ever since I was capable of reflecting on the subject, that those who can afford to pay for having their clothes, et cetera, made, defraud the industrious of what is their due, by making those articles themselves. I have also another odd fancy; I will not always employ those in the highest class of their profession, because, having some taste of my own, and not being very fond of finery, or going to the extreme of fashion, I can generally give such directions as shall cause my clothes to be made in a neat, becoming manner; and when I go to town, it will be time enough to purchase whatever splendid dresses I may require for making my entrance into the gay world, so as not to disgrace the family, or impeach the judgment of Mr. Franklin."

A month had flitted by on rapid wings, when, just at the close of a cold, dismal November day, as Franklin, having dined with the family at the rectory, was proposing a game of chess with Mr. Matthews, a letter was delivered to him by a servant, who said it was brought by one of Sir Robert Ainslie's grooms, who had ridden post from London, not stopping for anything but slight refreshment, and to change horses.

Lucy watched his countenance, as, having apologized to the company, he eagerly broke the seal and read it. The color fled from his cheeks; his lips quivered, and, putting his hand to his forehead, he faintly articulated,

"My poor father! my poor mother!"

"Are they ill? Has anything happened to either of them?" asked Lucy, as pale and agitated as himself.

"Something very dreadful has befallen them," he replied, "but of what nature, I cannot tell. These are a few, almost incoherent lines from Edward Ainslie, requesting I will not lose a moment in setting off for London. He will meet me a few miles from town, and explain what he did not choose to commit to paper. I shall set off for Southampton immediately on horseback, and from thence to my father's house as fast as a chaise and four horses can carry me."

"You will let us hear from you?" said Mr. Matthews.

"As early as the state of affairs will permit," was the reply.

"You know you have friends here who will not desert you in the day of adversity," said Mrs. Matthews, with one of her most benevolent looks.

The pale lips of Miss Blakeney moved, but no sound passed them; she held out her cold hand to Franklin, which having tenderly pressed, and respectfully kissed, he hastily said, "God bless you all!" and hurried out of the room.

In a moment his horse was heard going at a quick pace down the avenue, and anxiety and suspense became the inmates of the bosoms of Lucy and her sympathizing friends.

X

Manœuvring—establishment Formed— Change of Circumstances Alters Cases

It cannot be supposed but that, in the length of time elapsed since Lady Mary Lumly left the protection of her friends to trust to the honor of a profligate, many conjectures had been formed concerning her situation, and the treatment she met with from her husband. All the family at the rectory were anxious to hear from her, but how to direct their inquiries they were entirely at a loss.

Mr. Matthews once or twice called on Mrs. Brenton, but the old lady could give them no intelligence. The last letter she received from Theresa, was dated from Alnwick, and that was above seven months since; in that she said Sir Stephen and his lady talked of making a short trip to the continent, and if they invited her to accompany them, she should certainly go. The old lady did not express any uneasiness, concluding they were in France; and as Theresa never was a very attentive correspondent of her mother, she supposed her time was too much absorbed in pleasure to think much about her.

Mrs. Cavendish then wrote to some of Lady Mary' relations on the mother's side, to inquire if they had heard from her; but they, offended at her imprudent conduct, and the marriage connection she had formed, answered, that "They neither knew nor wished to know anything about her." The uneasiness of the family was much increased, when, a day or two after Mr. Franklin's departure, a gentleman lately returned from France called to deliver letters to Mr. Matthews, and, staying dinner, mentioned having seen Sir Stephen Haynes in Paris some little time since.

"Was his lady with him?" asked Mrs. Cavendish.

"There certainly was a lady with him," replied the gentleman, "but I did not understand she was his wife. I saw her several times, but never in his company. She was a bold-looking woman, of exceedingly free manners, and was said to lead a very gay life."

"That was not our poor Mary," whispered Aura to Miss Blakeney. Lucy shook her head, and the subject was dropped.

We left this victim of self-will and ill-directed sensibility at a cottage not many miles distant from Alnwick Castle, under the care of Mr. Craftly; but so ignorant were both Lady Mary and her friend of the country in which the cottage was situated, that they would have been unable to direct a servant, had any been allowed them, to find a post town or village by which means to transmit a letter to their friends. But for weeks after the departure of Sir Stephen, Lady Mary was in no state to write or hardly to think, being ill with a slow nervous fever, and at times delirious. Her highly excited state of feeling, her keen disappointment, added to a degree of self-accusation which her ingenuous mind could not suppress, was more than she could support, and she had nearly sunk under it—perhaps would have done so, but that Craftly, though he considered her as an imprudent young woman, pitied her sufferings, and interested his mother and sister in her behalf.

These truly virtuous and respectable women did not think that the commission of one fault was sufficient to banish a human being from society, or excuse in others the want of humanity or kindness. They went to the cottage; they hovered over her like guardian angels; and when, in her wanderings, she would call for Lucy, Aura, or Mrs. Matthews, they would one or the other present themselves at her bedside, soothe her administer her medicines, talk of Sir Stephen's return, of her reunion with her friends, and, by degrees, brought her back to health and a comparative degree of comfort.

Miss Brenton, taking her tone from these kind-hearted women, was tender and attentive. Lady Mary revived, as to external appearance, but her warm enthusiastic heart had been chilled, the bright prospects of youth to her were shrouded, and the sweet blossoms of hope were crushed forever.

Who and what was Craftly? A man of no mean capacity, nor bad feelings, who had been brought up to the profession of the law. He had lost his father early in life, but that father had secured to his wife and daughter, who was ten years the senior of her brother, a decent competency, and a genteel house in the vicinity of Alnwick. The residue of his estate and property he left to his son. There was considerable ready money. Craftly wished to taste the pleasures of a London season during that winter, but being young and inexperienced, he became the prey of sharpers and gamesters, and, among the rest, became a debtor to Sir Stephen Haynes. His money was run out; the few and trifling rents he had to receive had not become due, and the only security he had to offer was the mortgage of a small cottage and grounds he held in Northumberland.

When, therefore, Haynes met Craftly upon his return from the north with his newly made and lovely bride, it occurred to his unprincipled mind that he might make him subservient to his views in getting free from Lady Mary, and enjoying his intended tour to the continent in company with a dissolute woman, who had persuaded him, that though married and the mother of two lovely children, her invincible attachment to him had induced her to sacrifice all at the shrine of her illicit love.

This woman Sir Stephen Haynes had set up in his heart as a paragon of perfection; he did not feel that it was her blandishments that drew him first from the paths of rectitude; he did not know that a profligate, unprincipled woman, is the bane of man's peace, both here and hereafter.

Mary Lumly was agreeable in her person, sportive in her manners, and easily assailed by flattery. Her fortune had been represented as more than treble its value. He sought to obtain that fortune, but shrunk from proclaiming her as his wife. Possessed of her little patrimony, his thoughts reverted to the woman who had enslaved his youthful mind, and, leaving his confiding victim to what chance or time might produce, he took his adulterous paramour with him on his journey to France.

Lady Mary, recovered by the care of her unknown friends, began to think of living; and when she discovered she was likely to become a mother, life itself became more endeared to her. Lady Mary Lumly, however headstrong in her resolves, however misled by the spirit of romance and the flattery of pretended friends, had naturally a good heart, and an understanding above mediocrity.

The time she had passed in the family of Mr. Matthews had been of infinite service to her. The principles and habits of the individuals who formed that family, were such as had taught her, that the neglect of duty in others was no excuse for the same neglect in ourselves.

"I am forsaken," she mentally argued, "deceived, and plundered of fortune and good name; but if my misconduct is the cause of a human being coming into the world, a being dependent on me for everything, it is my duty to submit to the evils I have brought upon myself, and be to the little innocent, father, mother, all. How we are to be supported, God alone can tell; but my revered guardian used to tell me, that our Heavenly Father would maintain the cause of the orphan, and be the judge of the widow. Alas! for me, I am more desolate them a widow; my infant, if it ever sees the light,—unless his father be led to do us justice,—more wretched than an orphan."

It may be asked why she did not write to those friends she now knew how to appreciate. She did write, but Craftly had received orders to forward no letters whatever; he had therefore requested his mother and sister, before he agreed to their attending the sick-bed of Lady Mary, to give all letters, whether written by her or Miss Brenton, to him; alleging as a reason, that he could conveniently send them to the post-office, without trouble to them.

It may be remembered that Haynes had represented Theresa Brenton to Craftly, as an object, in regard to fortune, worthy of pursuit, and had intimated to that lady that Craftly was an independent man. A genteel establishment was the aim of the lady; a little ready money would be very acceptable to the gentleman; therefore mutual civilities, condescension, and uniform politeness, were scrupulously practised between them. He asserted that Sir Stephen Haynes said he was not the husband of Lady Mary; that she was a thoughtless, romantic girl of fashion, who was so madly in love with him, that she had thrown herself upon his protection, without waiting for those forms which her friends would have insisted on, and which he had no inclination to submit to.

Theresa knew this in part to be true; but she also knew that the marriage ceremony had passed at Gretna Green, and that Mary Lumly was in her own opinion, though perhaps not in the eye of the law, the wife of Sir Stephen Haynes. But Lady Mary was now poor; where was the use of her (Theresa) irritating Sir Stephen? it would do her poor misguided friend no good, and might be of injury to the plans she had formed for herself. Miss Brenton then became in externals an entire new character; she had entirely developed the pure, unassuming characters of Mrs. Craftly and her daughter. Brought up in the country, mixing with but little society, though that little was select; of plain, good understanding, they were urbane in their manners, without being highly polished, and very pleasant companions, without being thought wits, or aiming to appear deeply learned. Of strict principles, both as it regarded religious duty and moral rectitude; cheerful without levity, and grave without affected sanctity their own minds, actuated by unsuspicious simplicity thought no evil of others, until positive facts obliged them to believe it.

With the son and brother, they had ever lived in harmony; for he was the idol of both, and they either did not or could not perceive a fault in him. He, on his part, had so much regard for their peace, as to guard against any of his misconduct reaching them, or giving them any disturbance.

Theresa Brenton, then, appeared to this family everything that was amiable. She was conciliating to the Craftlys; would talk most sagely upon economy, domestic concerns, quiet seclusion, and love of mental improvement; and when the gentleman was present, would descant on the beauties of her mother's seat near Southampton, without betraying that it was only a hired place, and that its chief beauties consisted in the neat, snug appearance of a small house and the garden surrounding it, and a view of the bay from the upper windows. Then she would pathetically lament poor Lady Mary's misfortune, and speak of her as a young woman of impetuous feelings, which had never been kept under any restraint, concluding, with a sigh,

"She fully believes herself Sir Stephen's wife, and it will be as well not to contradict her; in her present delicate state of health, it might produce fatal consequences. Though, what is to become of her, I cannot think; for, by her not hearing from her friends, I fear they have cast her off. I myself feel uneasy sometimes at not hearing from my mother; but elderly persons are not very fond of writing, so I do not think so much of it as I otherwise should."

Lady Mary endeavored to obtain from Craftly her husband's address; but he always pretended that he believed him to be so unsettled that a letter would have little chance of finding him.

All letters addressed to any member of Mr. Matthews family were condemned to the flames, or thrown by in a drawer amongst waste paper; nor was he more careful of those written by Theresa to her mother, though, to own the truth, she did not trouble him with many. He well knew that to send intelligence to Mrs. Brenton was furnishing a direct clue to the discovery of Lady Mary; and this he had promised his friend Haynes should not be made in less than six months after his departure.

"Besides," thought Craftly, "Theresa might mention my attentions to her mother; and if I bring myself to marry the girl, I might be plagued from that quarter about a settlement, and subject myself to have inquiries made which it may be neither easy nor convenient to answer."

"I have been thinking, my dear Theresa," said he one evening, as, seated in the porch, they were enjoying the full splendor of a harvest moon, "I have been thinking and wishing—indeed it is the wish also of my mother and sister,—they think it would be for the happiness of all concerned,—to unite our hands, as I trust our hearts are already in unison with each other, and form our establishment before the winter commences."

He then proceeded to explain his actual fortune and his expectations, and made it appear that his annual income was above five hundred pounds a year; but in this he included the cottage, without one word of the mortgage which Sir Stephen Haynes still held; though he had agreed to give up the interest which might arise from it for eighteen months to come, if Craftly would oblige him in the manner we have already seen he did. Finding the lady silent, the lover then went on to say,

"You will have no objection, my dear girl, to making this cottage our residence for the present. My mother will undoubtedly give us an invitation to pass part of the winter with her in Alnwick, which I do asure you is a very lively and genteel place, affording many rational and pleasant amusements: the society they mix in, is of the most respectable class."

"I can have no objection to pass a few weeks or months with Mrs. and Miss Craftly," said Theresa, interrupting him: "but as to agreeing to make this Gothic cottage a place of residence, except for a few months, in the heat of summer, I can never agree to it. I expect, at least the first winter after our marriage, that you will permit me to partake, in your society, of the pleasures of either York or London. I should prefer the latter. Indeed, it will be almost impossible to give my little fortune into your hands without a journey to the metropolis; we can then also make a visit to my mother, who I am afraid must begin to think me very negligent."

"Well!" thought Craftly, "this is moderation with a vengeance! A winter in London! I have had enough of winters in London. I must persuade her out of this notion, or there is an end of the matter. She cannot be rich enough to justify such a piece of extravagance." Putting on, therefore, one of his most engaging smiles, he replied,

"But, my dear Theresa, have you duly considered the expense of a London winter, or even a winter in York? The whole of my yearly income would not pay our expenses, living in barely decent style. And though I do not know the amount of your fortune, yet I will take upon me to say, that the greater part of it might be run out in a single winter in London, without enabling either of us to be considered *somebody*. You are certainly too well versed in economy not to consider it better to spend only our income in cutting a good figure in the respectable town of Alnwick for many winters, than to spend half our fortunes in cutting *no figure at all* in the great city of London one winter. Think better of that project, I entreat you, my Theresa."

There was reason in this. Determined, however, not to be easily thwarted, she made some further attempts to carry her point; but, finding the gentleman growing rather cool and distant, during the several days that she held out, she prudently yielded, and the preparations for the marriage were commenced with great alacrity.

XI

Fruits of Error

Lieutenant Franklin did not meet his friend Ainslie on the road to London, as he had expected. On his arrival in town, he hastened to Portland Place. The blinds of his father's splendid mansion were closed, and everything about wore an aspect of gloom. The door was opened by a servant whose countenance indicated some terrible calamity.

Franklin hastened towards his mother's apartment, but was met on the stairs by one of his brothers, who had been summoned home from Eton. From him he learned that his father lay apparently at the point of death, having ruptured a blood-vessel: that his mother had been by his bedside almost incessantly, since the accident had happened, and that the whole family were in a state of the greatest alarm and trepidation.

As he entered the sick-chamber, the closed windows, the low whisperings of the attendants, the odors of medicinal preparations, and, most of all, an occasional stifled sob from one of the children, who was permitted to be in the apartment for a few moments, brought home to his bosom the conviction that he was about to become fatherless. He approached the bed. His father lay perfectly motionless and silent, with closed eyes, watched by the partner of all his sorrows, who bent over him like some kind angel, with a ministry unremitted and untiring. An indifferent gazer might have read, upon the marble forehead and classic features of the patient, noble and generous feelings, commanding talents—a promise of everything that was excellent in character and desirable in fortune—all blighted by once yielding to the impulse of guilty passion. The wife and the son saw nothing but the mysterious hand of Providence, visiting, with severest affliction, one whom they had ever regarded with reverence and love.

Franklin placed himself near the bed, and, pressing the hand of his mother, waited in unutterable suspense the moment when his father should awake. At length he slowly opened his eyes, and fixing them on his son with a faint smile, said, in a low voice, "My dear boy, I was this moment thinking of you. It gives me happiness to remember, how soon you are to be blest with the society of one you love, and who deserves your affection. I have not been so tranquil for years, as I am just now, in this thought. I wish that I could see her. I think I could read in her features the promise of your happiness, and then go to my account in peace."

Franklin pressed his father's hand. The big tears of mingled love, gratitude, and sorrow, coursed down his cheeks. He could not speak in reply. He saw by his father's countenance, that it was too late to comply literally with his request, but, in the same moment, it occurred to him that he could almost accomplish his wish, by showing him the miniature of Lucy's mother, which he had playfully taken from her on the day of his departure, and, in his haste and alarm at the sudden summons, had forgotten to restore.

"I have a picture of her mother," said he, putting his hand in his bosom, "it is a good resemblance of herself."

He drew forth the miniature, and held it up before his father, who rose up, seized it with a convulsive grasp the moment the light fell on the features, and looking upon the initials on the back of it, shrieked out—

"It is—it is come again to blast my vision in my last hour!—The woman you would marry is my own daughter!—Just Heaven!—Oh! that I could have been spared this!—Go, my son! go to my private desk—you will there find the records of your father's shame, and your own fate!"

Nature was exhausted by the effort. He fell back on the bed, supported by his trembling wife, and in a few moments the wretched Franklin, the once gay, gallant, happy Montraville, was no more.

XII

DISCLOSURES

The obsequies of Colonel Franklin were attended with the circumstances of pomp and state which his rank required, and the journals of the day proclaimed his patriotism and public worth, while his family mourned in secret over the ruin caused by his unbridled passions.

Closeted with his bosom friend, Edward Ainslie, young Franklin laid before him the manuscript which he had found by his father's direction. It had been written in a season of deep remorse, and its object was evidently to redeem from undeserved obloquy, the memory of the unfortunate Charlotte Temple, the mother of Lucy Temple Blakeney. Probably Colonel Franklin had intended to transmit it to her friends. Indeed, a direction to that effect was found on a loose paper, in the desk. He took the whole blame of her ill-fated elopement upon himself. He disclosed circumstances which he had discovered after her decease, which proved her faithfulness to himself; and lamented, in terms of the deepest sorrow, that it was in his power to make her no better reparation for all her love and all her injuries, than the poor one of thus bearing testimony to her truth and his own cruelty and injustice. He had never intended this paper to be seen until after his decease. He could not bear to make these full disclosures, and afterwards look upon the countenances of his children; and he mentioned, that the reason why he had so readily complied with the wish of a rich relation of his wife, that he should change his family name of Montraville for that of Franklin, was, that under that name he had taken the first step which destroyed his peace: to use his own forcible expression, "he would willingly have lost all recollection of what he was, and changed not his name only, but himself."

"Edward!" said the unfortunate youth, when the reading of this terrible record was finished, "I have disclosed to you the story of my ruined, blasted hopes. Receive this as the strongest mark of my friendship and confidence. Go to *her!*"—he could not utter the name of Lucy. "Tell these dreadful truths in such a manner as your own feeling heart shall direct. She is a Christian. This is her great trial, sent to purify and exalt her soul, and fit her for a brighter sphere of existence. I cannot—I dare not see her again. I cannot even give you for her any other message than a simple, heartfelt *'God bless her!'* I have caused myself to be exchanged into a regiment which is ordered to India, and tomorrow I bid farewell to England!"

Edward promised implicitly to obey his friend's directions; and receiving from him the fatal miniature, he took leave of him for that day, and returned to his father's residence to despatch a letter to Mr. Matthews, promising to be with him in a few days, and bring full intelligence of all that related to these unfortunate occurrences.

The next day he attended his friend for the last time, and witnessed the final preparations for his departure. There was a firmness, a sternness of purpose in Franklin's countenance, which indicated that his thoughts were fixed on some high and distant object; and though he spoke not of his future prospects, Edward, who knew the force of his character, mentally predicted that his name would be found in the records of military renown.

There was an impatience to be gone apparent in some of his movements, as if he feared to linger a moment on English ground. But this was inadvertently displayed, and he took leave of his mother, family, and friend, with that deep emotion which must ever affect a feeling heart on such an occasion.

Edward was surprised at one circumstance, which was, that Mrs. Franklin seemed to approve of her son's purpose to leave the kingdom. He had expected to find her very anxious to retain him, as a protector to herself. But he had not attributed to that lady all the judgment and firmness which belonged to her character. He had witnessed her enduring affection, and her noble example of all the passive virtues. Her energy and decision were yet to appear.

When the carriage, which bore his friend to the place of embarkation, had disappeared, he turned to the widow, and made a most cordial tender of his services in whatever the most active friendship could perform for her in her new and trying situation. He mentioned his purpose of going to Hampshire, and offered to return and await her commands as soon as the purpose of his journey was accomplished. This friendly offer was very gratefully acknowledged, but the tender of his services in the city was declined. It was not her purpose, she said, to remain in London: but should any circumstances occur which would render it necessary to avail herself of his kind offer, she should not fail to do it, in virtue of the claim which his friendship for her son gave her. At any rate, he should be apprized of the future movements of the family by someone of its members.

Satisfied with this arrangement, Ainslie retired.

XIII

An Arrival

It may well be supposed that the family at the rectory were in a state of great anxiety at the departure of Franklin. The air of mystery which attended his hasty summons to town, served to increase their distress. Lucy struggled, severely but vainly, to preserve an appearance of composure. Much of her time was spent in the retirement of her chamber; and when she was with the family, and apparently deriving a temporary relief from her sorrows by joining in the usual occupations of the busy little circle, a sigh would escape from her in spite of all her efforts to preserve an appearance of calmness.

It seemed to her that a known calamity, however terrible and irremediable in its nature, would have been much more easy to be borne than this state of suspense. Alas! she was soon, too soon, to be undeceived on this point.

The third day brought a hasty letter from Ainslie to Mr. Matthews, simply stating the sudden demise of Colonel Franklin, without any mention of the attending circumstances. This was a relief; a melancholy one, indeed, but still, Lucy felt it as a relief, because it seemed to set some bounds to her apprehensions. It seemed natural, too, that Ainslie should be employed to write at such a moment. The sudden affliction might have rendered Franklin incapable of the effort.

Lucy now awaited the result with comparative tranquillity.

But the second letter of Edward, written after the disclosure made by his friend, which spoke of "painful and peculiarly unfortunate circumstances, which he would explain on his arrival," threw her into a new state of suspense. Here was more mystery. The first letter which summoned Franklin away had appeared to be unnecessarily dark and doubtful. The last renewed all the wretched doubts and fears of Lucy.

On the second day after the receipt of this letter, Lucy was sitting alone by the parlor fire. It was late in the afternoon; Mr. Matthews and Aura were absent, administering to the wants of the poor, and distributing clothing to the destitute, in anticipation of the approaching inclement season. Mrs. Matthews and her sister were busied about their household affairs. Lucy was musing on the memory of past joys, and painfully endeavoring to conjecture the reason of Franklin's mysterious silence, when the door opened, and Edward Ainslie stood before her, haggard and weary with his journey, and evidently suffering under mental perplexity and distress. At that moment he would have given the world for the relief of Mr. Matthews' presence. He felt as though possessed of some guilty secret, and his eye was instantly averted when he met her searching glance. He had hoped to encounter someother member of the family first, and instantly felt his mistake in not having sent for Mr. Matthews to meet him elsewhere. But retreat was now impossible. He felt that he must stand and answer.

Lucy had advanced and presented her hand as usual, but with such a look of distressful inquiry as went to his inmost soul. With an old and tried friend like Ainslie, ceremony was out of the question.

"Where is *Franklin?* Is he well? Is he safe?"

"He is well. Be composed, Lucy. Do not look so distressed." Ainslie knew not what to say.

"Is he well? Then why—Oh, why are you alone, Edward?"

"There are certain painful circumstances, which have prevented his accompanying me. You shall know them—*but*—"

"Oh, tell, I entreat you, tell me all. I have borne this terrible suspense long enough. Any thing will be preferable to what I now suffer. I have firmness to bear the worst certainty, but I have not patience to endure these doubts. If he is lost to me, say so, I charge you."

There was a vehemence, a solemnity in her manner, an eagerness in her look, a deep pathos in her voice, which Edward could no longer withstand. He trusted to the strength of her character, and determined to disclose the worst. With averted eyes, and a low and hardly audible voice, he replied,

"Alas! he is indeed lost to you!"

She did not shriek nor faint, nor fall into convulsions, but, placing her hand upon her brow, reclined against the mantel-piece a moment, and then left the apartment.

Ainslie lost no time in finding Mrs. Matthews, and apprising her of what had passed, and that lady instantly followed her young friend to her apartment. She had over-estimated her own strength. The sufferings of this last week had reduced her almost to exhaustion, and this stroke completed the prostration of her system. A violent fever was the consequence, and for several days, her life was despaired of. The distress of Ainslie during this period may be imagined.

XIV

ACTIVE BENEVOLENCE, THE BEST REMEDY FOR AFFLICTION

O n Ainslie's communicating to Mr. Matthews the circumstances which he had learned from Franklin, and bitterly lamenting his precipitate disclosure of them to Lucy, that good man appeared anxious to alleviate his unavailing regret, and to bring forward every palliation for what, at the worst, was no more than an error in judgment. He could not permit his young friend to consider himself responsible for the consequences, since the stroke could not have been averted, and could scarcely have been made to descend more gently upon the heart of the devoted girl.

A further disclosure was yet to take place; and never, in the whole course of his ministration among the wounded spirits that had required his care and kindness, had this worthy pastor been more severely tried then on this occasion. He meditated, communed with his friends, and sought for Divine assistance in prayer; and when at last the returning health of his tender charge rendered it not only advisable but necessary that she should know the whole, he came to the trial with fear and trembling.

What was his joy to find that she received the disclosure, which he had so much dreaded to make, not with resignation merely, but with satisfaction! It brought a balm to her wounded spirit, to know that she had not been voluntarily abandoned—that the man on whom she had placed her affections had yielded to a stern necessity, a terrible fate, in quitting her without even a last farewell. She approved his conduct. She regarded him as devoted to his country, herself as set apart for the holy cause of humanity; and, in accordance with this sentiment, she resolved to pass the remainder of her life in ministering to the distressed, and promoting the happiness of her friends.

Nor did she delay the commencement of this pious undertaking. Aided by her revered friend the pastor, she entered upon her schemes of active benevolence with an alacrity which, while it surprised those who were not intimately acquainted with her character, and justified the exalted esteem of her friends, served effectually to divert her mind from harrowing recollections and useless regrets.

Among the earliest of her plans for ameliorating the condition of the poor, was the founding of a little seminary for the education of female children. She chose a pleasant spot near the rectory, a quiet little nook, embosomed among the wooded hills, and commanding a view of the village and a wide expanse of soft meadow scenery; and there she caused to be erected a neat little building, a specimen—one might almost say, a model of Ionic architecture. Its chaste white pillars and modest walls, peeping through the surrounding elms, were just visible from her own window; and many were the tranquil and comparatively happy moments which she spent, sitting by that window, and planning in her own mind the internal arrangement and economy of the little establishment.

She had it divided into several apartments, and placed an intelligent and deserving young woman in each, to superintend the different parts of education which were to be taught. In one, the most useful kinds of needlework; in another, the common branches of instruction in schools; and in another, the principles of morality, and the plainest truths and precepts of religion; while, over all these, there was a sort of High School, to which a few only were promoted, who gave evidence of that degree of talent and probity which would fit them for extended usefulness. These, under the instruction of the preceptress of the whole establishment, were to receive a more finished education than the rest.

Into every part of the arrangement of these matters Lucy entered with an interest which surprised herself. She delighted in learning the natural bent and disposition of the young pupils, and would spend whole hours in conversing with them, listening with a kind interest to their artless answers and opinions, and often discovering, or supposing that she discovered in them, the elements of taste and fancy, or the germs of acute reasoning or strongly inventive power.

But it was in developing their affections and moral capabilities that she chiefly delighted. This was a field of exertion in which the example of the patroness was of infinite value to the instructors. Her own education, her knowledge of human character and of nature, her cultivated and refined moral taste, and, above all, the healing and religious light, which her admirable submission to the trying hand of Providence had shed over the world and all its concerns, as they appeared to her view,—all these things served to fit her for this species of ministry to the minds and hearts of these young persons.

In these pursuits, it is hardly necessary to say, she found a tranquillity and satisfaction which the splendid awards of fortune and fame can never impart.

XV

Church and State

E dward Ainslie had finished his studies at the University, where he had so distinguished himself as to afford the most favorable anticipations of his future success. He was in some doubt as to the profession which he should embrace. Inclination prompted him to devote himself to the church. His father was anxious that he should become a political character; probably being somewhat influenced by an offer, which he had had from one of the ministry, of a diplomatic appointment for his son.

This interesting subject was under consideration at the very time when the events, which we have just been recording, transpired. Edward had returned to London after witnessing the perfect recovery of Lucy, and the discussion concerning his future career was renewed with considerable interest.

On the evening after his return, he was sitting in the parlor of his father's splendid mansion. All the family except his father and himself had retired. They lingered a few moments to confer on the old subject.

"Well, Edward," said his father, "I hope you are ready now to oblige our friends in a certain quarter, and strengthen the hands of government."

"Indeed, sir, my late visit to the country has served rather to increase my predilection for the life of a country parson."

"My Lord Courtly says it is a thousand pities your talents should be so thrown away; and though I should not regard the thing in that light, yet I think that your country has some claims upon you. Let the livings of the church be given to the thousands who are unfit for, or unable to attain the promotion that is offered to you. If you accept a living, it is ten to one you disappoint some equally worthy expectant."

"Perhaps I shall do the same if I accept this diplomatic appointment."

"Little danger of that, I fancy, when the appointment is so freely offered you—when, in fact, you are solicited to accept it. Let me tell you, Edward, you know not how splendid a career you may be refusing to enter upon."

"I fear, my dear father, that you have not duly considered the cares and anxieties of a political life. It is a constant turmoil and struggle for distinction. All the sterner feelings of our nature are brought into action.

All the generous emotions and amiable weaknesses of humanity are regarded as fatal to one's success. A blunder in state affairs is considered worse than a crime."

"I think there is no profession," said the baronet, "in which a crime is not more fatal to success, in the long run, than a blunder. However, we are wandering from the subject. In one word, Edward, I think that you may carry all your strict moral principles and your high and generous sense of honor into public life, without in the least endangering your success."

"What you say may be strictly true, sir, but I have feelings and partialities which cannot fail to prove a hindrance. I shall sigh for seclusion and domestic enjoyment amidst the splendor of foreign courts, and never pen a despatch to be sent to old England, without longing to see its fair prospects of green fields and smiling cottages. I love to converse with nature in her still retreats; and if I must mingle with my fellow-men, let it not be in the vain strife for power and distinction, but rather in the delightful intercourse of social life, or in the more interesting relation of one who cares for their eternal welfare. If I were rich, the character I should most wish to figure in, would be that of a useful, benevolent, and religious country gentleman; as the advice and instruction which I could thus impart, would not arise simply from official duty, and might be rendered doubly efficient by acts of benevolence. Since that may not be, I am content with the humbler office of a country parson."

At this period of the conversation a servant entered with a letter directed to the baronet, saying that it had been brought by an express. He opened it, and hastily running it over, exclaimed,

"Well, my boy, you can have your wish now. See there!" handing him the open letter.

It was from the executor of a distant relation, who had taken a fancy to Edward in his childhood, and had now bequeathed him the whole of his large estate, situated in the north of England.

Astonishment and gratitude to the divine Disposer of events were visible in the countenance of the youth, as he silently lifted up his eyes in thanksgiving.

After a few minutes' pause, his father said, "Well, you will visit your property immediately, of course?"

"Yes, sir; but I wish to visit Hampshire for a few days before I set off for the north." And so saying, he bade his father goodnight, and retired.

XVI

An Engagement

Before leaving London, Ainslie called at the late residence of Mrs. Franklin, and was surprised to find the house in other hands. On making further inquiries of his father, he learned that she had embarked for New York with the whole of her family. On reflection, he was satisfied that this was the most natural and proper course for her. America was the land of her nativity, and the scene of all the happiness she had enjoyed in early life—England, the country where she had known nothing but misfortune and trial. Her young sons, too, would be able to figure with great advantage in the new country; and its existing friendly relations with that to which her oldest son owed allegiance, prevented her feeling any uneasiness on the score of his present employment in the India service. Edward's father also informed him that Mrs. Franklin's affairs in England were intrusted to the most responsible agents.

Being satisfied that there was nothing further which friendship required of him in that quarter, he set out for Hampshire, with rather different feelings from those which oppressed him on his last visit there.

We will not attempt to analyze his feelings at this time; but rather follow him to the rectory, whither he hastened after a half-hour spent at his father's seat. On entering the parlor, he found Mrs. Matthews and Mrs. Cavendish, and learned from them that the young ladies were gone to visit Lucy's favorite school.

He determined to take a short cut to this place; and accordingly strolled along a shaded pathway which led from the garden towards the spot. The sun was just approaching the horizon, and shed a rich splendor over a pile of massy clouds which reposed in the west. As he passed rapidly along, a turn in the path revealed to him the solitary figure of Aura Melville, in strong relief against the western sky, as she stood on the edge of a bank, and gazed upon the last footsteps of the retiring sun. He approached unobserved, and, just as he was on the point of speaking, heard her say in a low voice, as though thinking aloud,

"How beautiful! How much more beautiful it would be, if a certain friend were with me to pronounce it so!"

Laying his hand gently upon her arm, he murmured in the same soliloquizing tone, "How happy should I be if I might flatter myself that I were that friend!"

She turned, and the "orient blush of quick surprise" gave an animation to her features, which made her lover own to himself that he had never seen her half so lovely.

We have already hinted at Aura's partiality for Edward, and when we apprize the reader that he had long loved her with a respectful and devoted attachment, which he had only been prevented from declaring by his dependent situation and uncertainty with regard to his pursuits in life, it will readily be supposed that they were not many minutes after this in coming to a perfect understanding.

With lingering steps, and many a pause, they turned towards the rectory, long after the shadows of twilight had begun to fall. The rapture of those moments; the ardent expressions of the youth; the half-uttered confessions, the timid glances and averted looks of the maiden, and the intervals of silence—silence full of that happiness which is never known but once—all these must be imagined by the reader.

On their arrival at the rectory, they found that Lucy, who had been left at the school by Aura, had returned by the more frequented road, and the family were waiting their coming, while the smoking tea-urn sent forth its bubbling invitation to the most cheerful, if not the most sumptuous of all entertainments.

XVII

Tea-Table Conversation

W ell, Edward," said the good rector, as he slowly dipped his favorite beverage, "this is an unexpected pleasure. I had supposed that the wishes of your father and the rhetoric of the minister had prevailed over your philosophical resolutions, and that you were already half-way to Saint Petersburg. Perhaps you are only come to pay us a farewell visit, and are soon to set off for the north?"

Indeed, sir," replied Ainslie, "I am soon to set off for the north, but shall hardly reach the court of the Czars this winter."

"To Berlin, perhaps?"

"Too far, sir."

"Peradventure to Copenhagen?"

"Hardly so far, sir, as the 'Land o' cakes an brither Scots.' I am to sojourn for the next few weeks among the lakes and hills of Cumberland."

"Cumberland!" exclaimed three or four voices at once.

"For what purpose can you be going to Cumberland?" said Lucy Blakeney, "I never heard of any court in that quarter except that of Queen Mab."

"I am going to look after a little property there."

"I never heard your father say that he owned any estates in Cumberland," said the rector.

"But my great-uncle Barsteck did. You remember the old gentleman who used to visit my father, and take me with him in all his strolls about the pleasant hills and meadows here. He has long been declining in health; and the letter which brought us the melancholy intelligence of his decease, brought also the info nation that he had remembered his old favorite. I could have wished to be enriched by almost any other event than the loss of so good a friend."

The remembrance of his relative's early kindness came over him with such force at this moment, that he rose and turned away to the window; and it was some minutes before he was sufficiently composed to resume the conversation, in which he informed his friends that he had given up all thoughts of public life, and resolved to devote himself to more congenial pursuits amidst the romantic scenery of the lake country.

It may readily be supposed that this determination was highly approved by the worthy pastor, and that in the private interview which he had with Edward the next day, it had no small influence in procuring his approbation of the suit which he then preferred for the hand of his fair ward.

After a few delightful days spent in the society of his friends at the rectory, Edward set forward on his journey to the north.

XVIII

An Adventure

Edward's estate was in the vicinity of the romantic vale of Keswick. The mansion-house lately inhabited by his uncle, was an old-fashioned but comfortable house, situated on the southern declivity of the mountain Skiddaw, with a beautiful garden, and extensive but uneven grounds, laid out in a style entirely suited to the surrounding scenery. The view from the balcony in front of the house, was one of singular beauty and sublimity. A long valley stretched away to the south, disclosing in the distance the still glassy surface of Derwentwater, and terminated by the bold and fantastic mountains of Borrodaile. On the east, the lofty steps of Wallowcrag and Lodore seemed to pierce the very heavens; whilst the towering heights of Newland bounded the view on the west, displaying the picturesque varieties of mountain foliage and rocks.

The cottages and farm-houses of his tenants were scattered about in such points of view, as to afford a pleasing sort of embellishment to the landscape. Many of them were constructed of rough unhewn stone, and roofed with thick slates; and both the coverings and sides of the houses were not unfrequently overgrown with lichens and mosses, as well as surrounded with larches and sycamores. Edward made it his first business, on his arrival, to visit his tenantry; and he found no little pleasure in studying the characters of these humble-minded persons, whose residence in this sequestered mountain region had preserved their primitive manners from the tide of refinement and corruption which had swept over less fortunate portions of the country.

As he was taking his customary ride on horseback one afternoon, he arrived at a part of his estate remote from the mansion-house, and where he had not before been, when he was struck with the picturesque appearance of one of the stone cottages which we have mentioned above.

It was of a very irregular shape, and seemed to have received additions and improvements from several generations of its occupants.

The orchard, too, had its trees of all ages, and one craggy-looking apple tree, which stood before the door seemed, by its accumulation of moss, and its frequently protruded dry branches, to be coeval with the house itself. There was a little garden, with its shed full of bee-hives, and its narrow beds of herbs and borders of flowers, and a small but noisy rill, that came dashing down from the rocks in the rear of the cottage, and sent a smile of verdure and a fairy shout of melody over the whole scene.

Edward alighted and entered the cottage, where he was received with a hearty welcome. The farmer himself was away among the hills; but the good dame was "main glad to see his honor, and hoped his honor was coming to live among them, as his worship's honor that was dead and gone had always done."

He assured her that such was his intention.

"I am glad your honor has come here this afternoon," she proceeded, "for more reasons than one. Your honor must know there is a poor distressed young creature in the other room, who wandered here yesterday after a weary long journey. She is come of gentle blood, and talks of her relations, who seem to be all lords and ladies. But, sure enough, the poor thing is quite beside herself; and a woful sight she was, when she came to our door yesterday, with nothing in the world but an open-work straw bonnet on her head, and a thin shawl over her shoulders, poor soul, in such a biting cold day! Would not your honor please to be so good as just to speak a kind word to her? I'm thinking she's come from the south, and would be cheered at the sight of one from her own part of the country, and of her own degree too."

It will be readily supposed that Edward expressed a desire to see her; and he was accordingly conducted from the neat sitting-room, into which he had first been invited, into a small back-room, where, to his no small astonishment, he saw, seated in an easy-chair by the fire, and attended by a little girl, the unfortunate Lady Mary, the wife of Sir Stephen Haynes.

Her attire consisted of a soiled travelling-dress which had once been rich and showy; her countenance though thin and wasted, was flushed and feverish; and there was a wildness in her eyes which told the saddest tale of all, that not only was the wretched lady for saken by friends and fortune, but at-least partially deprived of the blessed light of reason.

She started at the sight of Edward, and exclaimed, 'Ha! so you have come at last. Well, there, I have been crying here all this livelong morning! My husband the duke is to be beheaded on Tower Hill tomorrow morning for high treason! But," said she, grasping Edward's arm and whispering vehemently in his ear, "I came within an ace of being queen for all that."

"Then, too," she continued, weeping bitterly, "they have imprisoned me here, and the constable of the castle has taken away my jewels, and sent away my waiting-maid, and left nobody but this simple maiden here to attend upon me. I could have forgiven them all this, but they have taken away my child, my pretty boy, with his bright eyes and his golden locks. Oh, why do they let me live any longer!" And she wrung her hands as one not to be comforted.

"Poor creature!" whispered the good woman of the house, "she has not been so raving before."

"I am acquainted with the unfortunate lady," replied Edward, in a low voice, "but she does not seem to know me."

"Know you!" shrieked Lady Mary, catching his last words, "Yes, I do know you, Edward Ainslie, and I know, too, what you are come here for. You have come to preach to me on the folly of ambition—to upbraid me for deserting my friends and protectors. But you may spare yourself the trouble. I shall answer for all tomorrow. I will die with my husband."

She said this with great energy, and then, after pausing a moment and looking thoughtfully on the floor, she burst into tears again, exclaiming, "But my poor boy! what will become of him? I pray heaven they may not destroy him. Surely he has done no injury to the state. If the king could look upon his innocent little face, surely he would spare him!"

Edward, perceiving that his presence could be of no service to her, left the apartment, and directed that every attention should be paid to her, and promised ample remuneration to the family for their trouble. Then, hastily mounting his horse, he rode to the nearest medical attendant, whom he despatched to the cottage before he returned home.

XIX

The Consequences of Imprudence

For several days after the occurrence which we have described in the last chapter, Lady Mary continued in a high fever, and the physician gave little hopes of her recovery. Edward visited the cottage everyday to inquire after her, and was at length happy to learn, that by the unremitted kindness and care of the worthy family, she was safely past the crisis of her disorder, and that her reason was restored; but her weakness was such, that she had not been permitted to attempt giving any account of the manner in which she came into the miserable state in which she was found.

She was assured that she was under the care of a friend who had known her in early life, and would visit her as soon as her strength would permit. Satisfied with this assurance, she recovered rapidly, and, in a month from the time of Edward's first visit to the cottage, was able to sit up a great part of the day, and to receive a visit from him.

The interview, as may readily be supposed, was an affecting one to both parties. Poor Lady Mary seemed to be thoroughly humbled by misfortune, and was desirous of nothing so much as to see her early friends, and receive their pardon for her unworthy conduct in deserting them. Edward assured her that their affection for her was the same as ever; that they had regarded her as misled by designing and artful persons; and that nothing would afford them such heartfelt pleasure, as to welcome her once more to their hospitable home.

Thus soothed and encouraged, she informed him of the events which we have already narrated concerning her elopement, and the subsequent desertion of her husband. She proceeded to say that she had lost her child, a beautiful boy, born at the Gothic cottage of which we have so frequently spoken; that after the marriage of Craftly and Theresa, which, out of regard to that young lady's taste, was celebrated with considerable parade, she had continued to reside with them in the cottage, in a state of indescribable wretchedness, on account of the neglect of her husband.

She said, that one day, when the rest of the family were out on an afternoon visit, she went into one of the chambers to look for a book, which, Theresa had told her as she went out, might be found in a drawer there. She pulled out one drawer of the bureau after another, in vain, till she came to the lower one, which came out with considerable difficulty. When, at last, she succeeded in drawing it out, what was her astonishment to find a great part of the letters which she had written to her husband and friends, tumbled into it, after being broken open! There were a great many more letters, and some among them directed to Craftly, in her husband's handwriting.

Convinced that she was suffering by some vile conspiracy, she felt herself justified in taking the whole to her room, after first closing the drawer to avoid a speedy discovery.

Besides her own and Sir Stephen's letters, there were several of Theresa's to her mother. Before the family returned, Lady Mary had read through the greater part of them, and notwithstanding the bewildering and oppressive emotions which impeded her progress and distracted her mind, she was able to make out pretty clearly what her situation was.

Her husband was living in Paris, immersed in dissipation. Craftly had been instructed by him, and was repeatedly charged in the letters, to suffer no communication between her and her friends; and what shocked the unfortunate lady most of all, and deprived her of recollection for some moments, was a determination expressed in one of the letters never to see her again, accompanied with the declaration, that although she supposed herself so, she was not really his wife.

After recovering from her fainting fit, she hurried through the remainder of the letters, with many tears and many prayers to heaven for support.

"Never in my life," said she, "did I pass an afternoon of such complete and thorough wretchedness. I thought myself lost beyond all hope—surrounded by enemies, and without a single protector or friend. Before the family returned, I restored the greater part of the letters to the drawer; and when desired to join them at tea, I sent an excuse, and was glad to be left neglected and undisturbed in my room until the next morning.

"During this time I had considered all the circumstances of my situation. It was apparent, from the suppression of Theresa's letters, that she had not from the first been a full participator in the plot against me. Yet it was not possible for me to give her my confidence, now that she had become the wife of Craftly, who was the chief instrument of the conspiracy. The mother and sister of this hypocrite were so fully persuaded of his honor, that they would have considered me a maniac or a calumniator, if I had

SUSANNA ROWSON

disclosed the truth to them. I had found out by the letters that Craftly was paid for my support by my husband, who relinquished the interest of a mortgage on Craftly' estate as payment. This I regarded as a tacit acknowledgment that I was his wife. But the evidence of Theresa, which I supposed could be drawn from her at some future time by my friends, I considered of still greater value.

"I had no reason to fear that I should be left in absolute want, or that I should be treated with open unkindness by any of the family. But it was dreadful to me to know, that I was living under the roof of a man who had conspired to deprive me of everything that is valuable in life. I could not look upon him without a secret shudder running through my frame. After revolving the circumstances of my situation for several days, during which I with difficulty preserved an outward appearance of composure, I at length came to the resolution to seek shelter with Mr. Matthews, and endeavor to recover the favor of my relations.

"But how to effect my escape, with any prospect of reaching my friends, was a difficult question. I had no money nor jewels of any considerable value; but there were a few valuable laces, which I might dispose of for enough to defray my travelling expenses. I accordingly packed them up with great care; and, learning that there was to be a fair in the neighborhood, I determined to dispose of them there. On the morning of the fair, I informed the family that I intended to take a walk, and spend the day in visiting the cottages in our neighborhood;—I hope the deception will be forgiven me. I put on my travelling-dress, concealed my treasure, and set forward, with mingled emotions of gladness and apprehension. I sold the laces without difficulty, though for considerably less than their value; and I have reason to believe that I was mistaken for one of those persons who gain a subsistence by smuggling articles of this kind from the continent. This, however, was a trifling consideration; I could have consented to pass for a gipsy or a fortune-teller, in order to escape from my persecutors.

"My next object was to secure a passage in the mail-coach which went south. Here was a greater trial of my courage; since this exposure was a continued one, while my other was but momentary. I played my part, however, as confidently as I could; and although my unprotected state exposed me to suspicions which the innkeeper, his wife, and even the servants were at no great pains to conceal, yet I was enabled to bear up against it all, without a tear, and arrived at the end of the first stage without any accident.

"The fatigues of the last two days, however, were so great, that I was nearly overcome when we arrived at the inn which was at the termination of this stage, and I retired to a room apart, as soon as we arrived. I observed a newspaper lying in the window-seat, and after refreshing myself with a cup of tea, I took it up, half-hoping to see the name of some friend in its columns. Judge of my horror on reading the fatal record of my husband's death. He had fallen in a duel in Paris. I had loved him—Oh, too well!"

Here Lady Mary became too much affected to proceed with her narrative. Indeed, she had little more to relate; for the shock had proved too great for her reason, and from that moment she recollected little more than that she had wandered from village to village, pitied and relieved by some, and derided by others, until she found herself in her present asylum, restored to perfect recollection by the care of the good people around her.

Edward had listened to her narrative with the deepest interest and compassion, and assured her of the protection and support of her *friends*, whatever might be the determination of her relatives. He gave directions for her further accommodation at the cottage during her convalescence, and it was arranged that as soon as her strength would permit, she should take up her residence at his own house.

Having been delayed only by his desire to learn all that related to her, and to provide for her comfort, Edward set off for the south as soon as these arrangements had been completed, leaving Lady Mary under the care of the worthy family at the cottage.

XX

An Old-Fashioned Wedding

The time would fail us to enumerate the multiplied works of charity in which Lucy Blakeney employed herself. She was not content with occasionally visiting the poor and administering to their more urgent wants; but she made the true economy of benevolence her study. Her knowledge, her taste, her wealth, were all rendered subservient to the great cause. Without officiously intermeddling with the charities of others, she became a bright example to them. Her well-timed assistance was a stimulus and an encouragement to the industrious poor, and her silent and steady perseverance was a strong appeal to the better feelings of the rich. She received the blessing of him that was ready to perish, and the unheard praise and unsolicited imitation of those who had abundance of wealth and influence.

As the nuptials of her friend Aura Melville approached, her attention was directed to the proper mode of honoring that event, and at the same time rendering it memorable among those who had long regarded both these young persons as the joint guardians of their happiness. Mr. and Mrs. Matthews, and Mrs. Cavendish, too, desired to have the marriage celebrated after the fashion of the good old times, when the poor not only looked up to the gentry for protection and friendship, but took a lively interest in their domestic affairs, and were both depressed at their misfortunes, and proud and happy in the fame and happiness of their patrons.

Nor was Edward Ainslie backward in promoting this design. Accordingly, the preparations for the marriage were made with a view to interest and gratify rather than to dazzle the guests. The bridal array was rather plain than sumptuous; the carriages and horses of Edward and his family were decked with ribbons, and the church ornamented with flowers and evergreens, prepared by the pupils of Lucy's establishment, who also walked in procession, and had their dance upon the green, to the music of the pipe and tabor. The villagers crowded the church to witness the ceremony, and repaired to the rectory to partake of the bride-cake, while the poor who had been invited to celebrate Lucy's birth-day, found an entertainment not less substantial and exhilarating than the former one, prepared for them at her friend's wedding.

A long summer's day was spent in the festivities of this happy occasion; and when, late in the evening, the full moon was seen rising behind the church tower, and shedding her quiet lustre over hill and valley, streamlet and grove, the music was still sounding, and the merry laugh of the light-hearted guests was heard in parlor and hall.

None seemed to enjoy the day more deeply and feelingly than Lucy. She had learned the great secret of woman's happiness, to enjoy the happiness of others. Selfish gratification was no concern of hers. She had entered into the previous arrangements with all her heart; and as her object had been, not to lay her friends under heavy obligations, and astonish the guests by show and parade, but to promote the zeal and heartfelt pleasure of all concerned, she succeeded; and none derived more satisfaction from partaking of this festival of true joy that she did from its preparation.

When, on the following morning, Edward and his bride set off for the north, she, with the rest of the family, bade them a tender adieu, and returned to her usual benevolent occupations with that tranquil and calm spirit, that firm reliance on the righteous Dispose of all things, which, in every situation of life, is indeed the pearl of inestimable value.

Conclusion

S everal years rolled away after the event recorded in the last chapter, without affording anything worthy the attention of the reader. The persons to whom our narrative relates, were enjoying that calm happiness which, as has frequently been remarked, affords so little matter for history. We must accordingly conclude the story with the incidents of a somewhat later period.

It was the season of the Christmas holidays. Edward and his blooming wife, with their two lovely children, were on a visit to his father, and had come to pass an evening at the rectory. Lady Mary, too, was there. She had recovered from the wreck of her husband's property enough to support her genteelly, and had found an asylum with her old preceptor and guide, in the only place where she had ever enjoyed anything like solid happiness.

The rector, now rapidly declining into the vale of years, afforded a picture of all that is venerable in goodness; his lady retained her placid and amiable virtues, although her activity was gone; and the worthy Mrs. Cavendish, still stately in her carriage, and shrewd and decisive in her remarks, presented no bad counterpart to her milder sister.

Last, but not the least interesting of the cheerful group which was now assembled around the fireside of the rector, was Lucy Blakeney. Her beauty, unimpaired by her early sorrows, and preserved by the active and healthful discharge of the duties of benevolence, had now become matured into the fairest model of lovely womanhood. It was not that beauty which may be produced by the exquisite blending of pure tints on the cheek and brow, by fair waving tresses and perfect symmetry of outline; it was the beauty of character and intellect, the beauty that speaks in the eye, informs every gesture and look, and carries to the heart at once the conviction, that in such a one we behold a lovely work of the Creator, blessed by his own hand, and pronounced good.

The rector was delighted to find the three orphans once more met under his own roof, and apparently enjoying the blessings of this world in such a spirit as gave him no painful apprehensions concerning the future.

"I cannot express to you," he said, "how happy I am to see you all here again once more before my departure. It has long been the desire of my heart. It is accomplished, and I can now leave my blessing with you, and depart in peace."

"You cannot enjoy the meeting more highly than we do, I am sure," said Aura. "The return to this spot brings back a thousand tender and delightful associations to my mind; and I regard among the most pleasing circumstances which attended our meeting, the degree of health and enjoyment in which we find all our old friends at the rectory. But how do all our acquaintances among the cottagers? Is the old serjeant living?"

"He is in excellent health," replied the rector, "and tells all his old stories with as much animation as ever."

"And your little proteges, Lady Mary, the distressed family which you found out?" rejoined Aura.

"They are well, and quite a happy, industrious family," answered Lady Mary, with a slight blush.

"How goes on the school, Lucy?" said Edward. "I regard that as the most effective instrument of benevolent exertion."

"I hope it has effected some good," answered Lucy. "There have been a considerable number from the school who have proved useful and respectable so far; several of the pupils are now married, and others are giving instruction in different parts of the country. A circumstance which has afforded us considerable gratification is, that a pupil, whose merit has raised her to a high station in life, has visited us lately, and presented a handsome donation towards rendering the establishment permanent."

After a short pause in the conversation, Mr. Matthews expressed a wish that they might have some intelligence from their absent friends.

"I have this day received a letter from America," said Edward, taking it from his pocket and looking inquiringly at Lucy.

"I think you may venture to read it to us," said she.

It was from Mrs. Franklin, and informed him that she had purchased a beautiful seat on the banks of the Delaware, and was living there, in the enjoyment of all the happiness which was to be derived from the society of her family and the delightful serenity of nature. One circumstance only had happened since her departure from England to mar this enjoyment, the account of which must be given in her own words.

"My eldest son, your friend—no doubt you have often heard from him. He soon grew tired of the India service, and was at his own desire exchanged into a regiment which had been ordered to join the army in Spain. There his career was marked with the heroism and generosity which had ever distinguished his character. A young officer is now visiting me, who accompanied him in his last campaign. He informs me, that my noble son never lost an opportunity either of signalizing himself in action, or relieving the distresses of those who suffered the calamities of war.

"In one of the severest battles fought upon the Peninsula, it was the fortune of my son to receive a severe wound, while gallantly leading his men to a breach in the walls of a fortified town. The English were repulsed, and a French officer, passing over the field, a few hours after, with a detachment, had the barbarity to order one of his men to fix his bayonet in him. His friend, who was also wounded and lay near him, saw it, but was too helpless himself to raise an arm in his defence.

"The same night, the town was taken by storm. When the English force advanced, the unfortunate officers were both conveyed to safe quarters, and my poor son lived thirty-six hours after the capture of the place. During this time, the story of his inhuman treatment reached the ears of the commander-in-chief. Fired with indignation, he hastened to the quarters of the wounded officers.

"'Poor Franklin,' says his friend, 'was lying in the arms of his faithful servant, and breathing heavily, when the illustrious Wellington entered the room. It was apparent to all that he had but a few moments to live.

"'Tell me,' said the general; 'exert but strength enough to describe to me the villain who inflicted that unmanly outrage upon you, and I swear by the honor of a soldier that in one hour his life shall answer for it.'

"'Never did I see the noble countenance of Franklin assume such an expression of calm magnanimity as when he replied,

"'I am not able to designate him; and if I could do it with certainty, be assured, sir, that I never would.'

"'These were his last words, and in a few minutes more his spirit fled to a brighter region.'"

If there are sorrows which refuse the balm of sympathy, there are also consolations which those around us "can neither give nor take away." Through the remaining years of her life, the orphan daughter of the unfortunate Charlotte Temple evinced the power and efficiency of those exalted principles, which can support the mind under every trial, and the happiness of those pure emotions and lofty aspirations whose objects are raised far above the variable contingencies of time and sense.

In the circle of her friends she seldom alluded to past events; and though no one presumed to invade the sanctuary of her private griefs and recollections, yet all admired the serene composure with which she bore them. Various and comprehensive schemes of benevolence formed the work of her life, and religion shed its holy and healing light over all her paths.

When the summons came which released her pure spirit from its earthly tenement, and the history of her family was closed with the life of its last representative; those who had witnessed, in her mother's fate, the ruin resulting from once yielding to the seductive influence of passion, acknowledged, in the events of the daughter's life, that benignant power which can bring, out of the most bitter and blighting disappointments, the richest fruits of virtue and happiness.

THE END

A Note About the Author

Susanna Rowson (1762–1824) was a British-American novelist, poet, actress, and geographer. Born in Portsmouth, England, Rowson was taken to Massachusetts by her father, a Royal Navy officer, following the death of her mother. The family was placed under house arrest during the American Revolution and moved from Nantasket to Abington, Massachusetts. In 1778, they were sent to Halifax, Nova Scotia as part of a prisoner exchange and later settled in Yorkshire, England. As a young woman, Susanna moved to London and embarked on a career as a writer with the publication of *Victoria* (1786). Five years later, she published *Charlotte Temple*, which went on to become the first bestselling novel in the newly formed United States. In 1793, after gaining a reputation as an actress in Edinburgh, Susanna moved to Philadelphia to join the theater company of Thomas Wignell, for whom she performed over fifty roles in just two seasons on stage. She left theater several years later to found a school for girls in Boston, which she later moved to Newton, Massachusetts. Rowson continued writing works of fiction throughout her life, but largely devoted herself to education in her late career. *Rowson's Abridgement to Universal Geography* (1805) and *Youth's First Steps in Geography* (1811) are considered the first works of human geography—incorporating social and religious subjects—published in history. She ran her school, which eventually returned to Boston, until 1822, at which point she retired and handed operations over to her daughters.

A Note from the Publisher

Spanning many genres, from non-fiction essays to literature classics to children's books and lyric poetry, Mint Edition books showcase the master works of our time in a modern new package. The text is freshly typeset, is clean and easy to read, and features a new note about the author in each volume. Many books also include exclusive new introductory material. Every book boasts a striking new cover, which makes it as appropriate for collecting as it is for gift giving. Mint Edition books are only printed when a reader orders them, so natural resources are not wasted. We're proud that our books are never manufactured in excess and exist only in the exact quantity they need to be read and enjoyed.

bookfinity™

Discover more of your favorite classics with Bookfinity™.

- Track your reading with custom book lists.
- Get great book recommendations for your personalized Reader Type.
- Add reviews for your favorite books.
- AND MUCH MORE!

Visit **bookfinity.com** and take the fun Reader Type quiz to get started.

Enjoy our classic and modern companion pairings!

Classic & Modern

Printed in the USA
CPSIA information can be obtained
at www.ICGtesting.com
JSHW080002150824
68134JS00021B/2229